LEGEND OF THE FALCON PRINCE

THE HEXIUM
BOOK ONE

S.JUDITH BERNSTEIN

Published 2024 by Trickster Cat Publishing .LLC

Legend of the Falcon Prince

For more information please contact
https://www.trickstercatpublishing.com/contact
Library of Congress Cataloging-in-Publication Data is available
ISBN 978-1-959825-02-9 (paperback)
ISBN 978-1-959825-03-6 (ebook)

For Claire

For forcing me to eat and sleep and even take the occasional break while writing this.

CONTENT WARNING

Violence, blood and injury, on page murder (of an antagonist), death of a horse (off page, implied), death of a close family member (off page, remembered)

MADRIA
MIRIDIAM OCEAN
TALAY
PALIA
SINOTALYA
CYLBRIN MOUNTAINS
TU MYDE
FY DOR
FROSTBOR RIVER
LOTH TEL
LOTH TEL LAKE
KAY WEN
H'ARN
WY DEL
BLUE RIVER
COR NIVAR
ADREN MOUNTAINS
KILANIAN RIVER
TAR MEL
SKYSTONE MOUNTAINS
CAR CULOND
MEL TIMEDEN
MI LOR
EL AMARDEN
DUCHY OF YINGTIAN
ESTRON
THE CATIAN OCEAN
THE CATIAN OCEAN

"There is a god of battles, of war and victory and justice writ in blood. She who shapes the world on her blade and carves fate as she sees fit. She is made from the night with the stars as her eyes and a sword in her hand. Bands of starlight wrap her arms and crown her brow, and her star sign is the divinity of she and her. She is Adjra, the Queen of Battle, and she waits in the knife and the sword, and the wrongs that only blood can right."

-The Hexium: Book of the Divine

PROLOGUE

The girl ran through the burning world. Her every breath tore at her lungs, filling them with smoke and soot and the scent of the end of everything. The city was burning, her city, her city where she laughed and played and ran. The girl liked to run, she liked the feel of the speed, the stretch in her legs, the wind tangling in her hair, but now the wind was ash and the ground was too hot and the tears in her eyes blurred the familiar street into unfamiliar nightmare.

Her name was Dawn, a name of new beginnings, given to her by her parents in hopes that she would be born into a better world, that the fighting was at an end and peace would finally come to Avarniy, and it had come. Briefly. In guarded borders and careful watching and an alliance with H'arn, the great power at the center of the continent which promised aid and shared defense against the threat of invasion from southern Estron. Yet now that peace was wiped away, blotted from the world as though it had never been. The tide of violence known as the Crimson Age was washing over Avarniy, and Avarniy was being swept away, drowned in an ocean of flames and ash and blood.

Don't think about the blood.

Don't think about the blood.

Don't think about Avery.

Don't think about mothers.

Don't think about.

Don't think about.

Don't think about.

There was so much blood. It splattered the floor, the walls, the garden path. Even Dawn hadn't been spared. She could feel it now, drying sticky and wrong against her skin, but she couldn't think about that, couldn't think about whose blood, couldn't think about... Couldn't think about anything.

She couldn't think.

If she thought the tears would become too much and she wouldn't be able to breath the smoky air and she wouldn't be able to run and she needed to run, run, run. It was all she could do. Run and find Lyra, run, find the bird, find the last little bits of the world that hadn't already burned.

It shouldn't have been like this. None of it should have been like this. Dawn wanted to scream the words into the burning night but there was no breath left in her for such things. Why hadn't they come? Why? Why? WHY?

For three years the alliance had stood, for three years H'arn and her own beloved Avarniy had guarded each other's boarders, protected each other's interests, stood together against Estron. But Estron wasn't the source of this burning, Palia was. The large nation to Avarniy's north had crossed the border and swept downward in a single deadly strike, burning away the world all around it until they came to the capital, and H'arn... Where was H'arn? Their strongest ally, their friend, their defender to the north and west who should have made sure that Palia would never dare something like this. Where were they??

Where? Where? Where? Dawn's heart seemed to pound the question with every desperate beat as she finally reached the sun tower and darted inside. The air was slightly better in the tower, the thick stone blocking out the worst of the smoke, and part of Dawn wanted to collapse right there, let the cool stone and the familiar dark take her. Maybe if she did this would all be a dream. Maybe if she did she would wake in her own bed with Avery shaking her shoulder or one of her mothers bending over her, asking her how she had managed to oversleep when she was usually the first one awake, maybe...

Maybe.

"Please..." The word left her cracked lips in a desperate prayer to the Star Fox, the god of peace and mercy. *Please let this be a dream. Please let this be a nightmare. Please. Please. Please...*

Yet even as she prayed she began to climb, dragging her exhausted body up step after step of the never ending spiral of the sun tower, because this wasn't a dream. Too real, too horrible, too much. She could never even have imagined something like this, could never have imagined Avery and mother and mother and... No, don't think about the blood, don't think about the blood, don't think about it don't think about it don't think about it.

Somehow Dawn made it to the top of the tower. Somehow she pulled herself to the edge of the room and looked down through the great open sides of the tower down into a sea of fire. Avarniy was burning. It's proud wooden houses, its shops and market stalls, even its famed gardens—all gone, all nothing but an ocean of flame. And there was nothing Dawn could do, not to save her people, not to save her family, not to save anyone. Nothing except...

A shrill cry rang from above her, different from the screams echoing up from below the tower. This wasn't anger or human agony. This was the harsh demanding call of a bird who did not like the taste of smoke in her lungs, and it was the only sound that could drag one last bit of effort from Dawn. It was the reason she had come.

"Get help! Send Lute! Hurry! Run!"

Avery's final command before she'd thrown herself, sword drawn, in front of that Palian soldier, and so Dawn had run, run through her tears, through the flames, through all of it, because if there was any chance at help, it was this. Dawn held up her hand and the small red-brown Summer Hawk landed on her arm. She hadn't been the one to train the bird, she wouldn't have the first clue how, but Dia was good with birds, no Dia was the *best* with birds, and if she told Lute to find him then find him she would.

...But find him with what? It was only then that Dawn realized that she had no paper, no pen, no way to send a message. It was... It was for nothing...

The sight of Avery throwing herself in front of that soldier flashed through Dawn's thoughts again, quick and painful and scalding as a brand.

No, she couldn't let it be for nothing. She couldn't. She wouldn't.

Moving quickly, Dawn shifted Lute to a nearby perch then pulled the dagger from her waist and cut an uneven chunk of fabric from her tunic. The formerly white fabric was stained by ash and blood but it would have to do. No it *would* do. Now for ink... This part was harder but once again the memory of Avery's final moments burned through her mind and with a hiss of pain and a muffled sob Dawn slashed the blade down the side of her arm. The cut hurt but she did her best to ignore it, dipping a finger into the wound and coating its tips in blood. It was not enough for anything long, it would dry too fast for that and if she cut herself again she could lose too much blood and be unable to search for Lyra. As she sat choaking back sobs in the tower at the center of her burning world, Dawn traced two words onto the fabric in her own blood.

"Help us."

CHAPTER I

THE FALCON

Until the moment he felt his foot slip against the wet roof tile, Dia thought he was going to get away. He'd managed to make it down the tree and across the queen's garden before the guards caught up with him. The small wall door had still been propped open just as he had left it and once he was out into the Palace City beyond it all he needed to do was find a place to hide. He'd known that he wouldn't be able to keep ahead of the guards for much longer, his body just wasn't built for this sort of running. Already he could feel the ice burn pain in his ears and at the tip of his nose which told him that his blood was no longer flowing to all of the places it should be. But even as he reached the end of his endurance he still thought that he was going to get away. The climb to the low roof of the messenger building was easy with practice, the pile of crates by its eastern wall offering a familiar path even in the dark and the rain. All Dia had to do was reach the open slats of the aviary dome and slip between them before the guards saw him on the roof and he would be safe.

That was when Dia heard the sound behind him, the

creek and clatter of someone following his path onto the roof. The guards were still behind him, farther back and shouting. Maybe one had gotten closer than he thought and maybe all he heard was the storm, but either way Dia put his head down and tried to move faster. The roof of the messenger building was like every other roof in the Palace City, low and gently sloping and made from gray slate. There was a trick to balancing on it, a way to plant one's feet at just the right angle and tilt one's body so that the wind was his friend instead of his enemy. Maybe it wasn't a risk he should have taken in the rain, but with the way his heart was racing and his ears were burning Dia would never have been able to escape the guards on foot. Too much longer running along the ground and he would have collapsed, unable to even defend himself when the guards did inevitably find him. And if they found him...

If they found him...

Dia threw himself forward in a final burst, hooking his right arm around the side of one of the beams which made up the 'bars' of the giant birdcage shaped aviary. He was just bringing his left arm up to rest on one of the aviary's low walls in preparation for vaulting himself over it and into safety when everything went wrong. His boot struck the tile but the angle was off, the water-slick slate sliding from beneath his heel. Dia was good at walking the palace roofs, good at the tricks of balance and motion which let him move unnoticed through the night-dark city. Normally he could've corrected, could have saved himself, but he was moving too fast. The momentum which should have seen him tumbling safely into the aviary tore the tile from beneath his foot and there was no time, no time to catch his balance, no time to keep his other foot from slipping as well. Pain ripped through Dia's shoulder as the arm he'd wrapped around the aviary's slat suddenly became the only thing keeping him on the roof. Desperately his feet scrabbled against the slate, trying to find purchase, his left hand fumbled against the aviary wall, searching for a grip, for leverage, for anything that would let him save himself.

Not like this...

Not like this...

Not...

Suddenly a hand closed around Dia's right arm, yanking him toward safety. Dia didn't pause to question it, he just brought his slipping feet down as hard as he could against the tile. One foot caught the edge of the roof and he pushed off of it, using the momentum to shove himself upward toward whoever was trying to help him. His rescuer seemed to not be expecting that, and for a horrible moment he thought they would overbalance down the other side of the roof. Then they were turning slightly, momentum carrying them backward between the slats, and Dia and his rescuer collapsed in a heap on the aviary floor.

For a moment all Dia could do was lay there, gasping, heart racing and body half-sprawled over whoever it was who had saved him. So close, he had been so close...

"What was that?"

"Sounded like it came from the messenger building!"

"Check the aviary!"

Guards' voices drifting up from below brought the panic back and Dia scrambled to his feet, fast. Too fast. The world spun and for an instant everything went black.

"What's wrong?"

The question came just as Dia fell against one of the slats. The voice was a light tenor, curious, urgent and utterly unfamiliar.

"It's nothing." Dia peered into the darkness, but even as

his heartbeat settled and the threat of unconsciousness withdrew he could still see nothing. The shadows of the aviary were too deep and clouds blotted out the moon and stars.

"Get the door open!" The call came from just below them followed by the sounds of someone fumbling with the lock.

Dia stiffened. He was out of options. There was no way he would be able to escape this, not trapped up here, not with a witness who must have seen his flight.

"Lose the cloak." The voice came quick and urgent through the darkness.

What-

Oh!

The implication of the words clicked into place and Dia moved, untangling the gray rain cloak from around himself. Tossing it into a pile behind him, Dia backed against the nearest slat so that the shadow of his body would hide the fabric from at least a cursory look. Below him he heard the messenger building's door slam open, heard boots rushing for the stairs, and then there was a hand on his shoulder and another tangling in his hair, using it to drag his head downward. Dia only had time for a startled gasp then a pair of soft lips was pressing against his own.

For a moment all Dia could do was freeze, shock and panic warring in him. He could feel the stranger's body against his own, feel his warmth, the wetness of his clothes, the pressure of his lips. It was a strange intimate feeling, foreign and unexpected, and Dia's first instinct was to push the stranger away but he caught himself, his arms snapping up instead to wrap around the other's body. Just in time. The aviary trapdoor slammed open, lantern light and guards streaming through it, and Dia and the stranger jumped apart, forming a realistic picture of interrupted lovers.

"What the..."

"Your Highness!"

Dia's heart was pounding, his head spinning, but that was fine. No matter what his expression showed, the guards would only think it was a response to being interrupted. They had come here chasing one man, they would not have been expecting to find two. Above him in their nests the falcons, roused from sleep by the sudden light and noise, let out shrill irritated calls. One, a White Peaks falcon, actually spread her wings and dove shrieking toward the guards who had frozen around the mouth of the trapdoor, staring at Dia and his companion. As the falcon swept toward them the guards jerked back, throwing up their hands protectively and sending their lantern swinging wide and wild.

"Frost!" Dia threw out an arm and the large Peaks falcon broke out of her dive with an irritated cry before circling down to land on the offered perch. Dia felt the prick of talons against his skin as they locked around his arm but it was a familiar pain, comforting, exactly what he needed to ground himself and take control of the moment.

"What is this?" Dia stepped forward toward the guards whose eyes were still fixed warily on the murderous bird now seated comfortably on Dia's forearm. Hastily their eyes snapped from falcon to master and they drew themselves up as though presenting a formal report.

"Sorry for the disturbance, Your Highness, but we were chasing a spy."

"A spy?" Dia let his eyes widen and his shoulder stiffen and was rewarded by three nods of confirmation.

"In the Queen's garden. We chased them into the Palace City."

"Have you seen anything, my lord?"

"We were a bit too busy for that, don't you think?" The answer came smug and amused, and Dia couldn't help turning quickly to glance at the speaker.

The man standing beside him was dressed in the gold buttoned black short coat of the royal guard. He looked young, perhaps even a year or two younger than Dia's own twenty- one years and he was a few inches shorter than Dia but something about the length of his torso— or just the way he held himself still— seemed to suggest height. His skin was southern pale and his hair was a red orange flame, hanging loosely half out of the ponytail which had once restrained it. Dia guessed that it had come free during their struggle with gravity but the guards would probably think... Well, it would help with the ruse and that was all that mattered.

"You, don't I know you?" It was the guard with the lantern who asked the question, eyes narrowing as they focused on the stranger, the respectful tone he had been using on Dia dropping away the moment he began speaking to one of his own.

Quickly Dia cleared his throat, dragging all eyes back to him. "If you three are supposed to be catching a spy then what are you doing here?"

Dia took a step forward as he spoke, half shielding the other man behind him. It wasn't that he actually felt anything protective. The man was a stranger after all, but if this really was his lover then this was how he would be expected to react, and it let him take back control of the conversation.

Instantly all three guards stiffened.

"Well?" Dia demanded.

"Forgive the interruption, Your Highness." The lead guard bowed his head. "We had better continue searching." The other two guards inclined their heads as well, and then all three turned and retreated through the trapdoor.

Dia waited in silence as he listened to their footsteps on the stairs below. On his arm Frost shifted restlessly from foot to foot, her talons continuing to dig their way through his sleeve and into his skin. His mother wasn't going to be pleased when she found that he had let the falcon ruin yet another shirt. It was an abstract thought but a familiar one and it helped to calm Dia's racing mind. At last, when he heard the door of the messenger building shutting again behind the guards and they were alone with the birds and the rain and the night, the prince turned to the man beside him and asked, "What's your price?"

CHAPTER 2
THE FOX

"Can't you guess?" The question held a hint of a smile in it, perhaps mocking, perhaps only teasing. In the renewed darkness it was hard to tell.

"Money or a promotion?" Dia asked. They were the most obvious options when it came to blackmailing a prince; they would also be nearly impossible for him to grant. Hopefully the stranger would know that. Dia's status in the court was as well-known as his face was recognizable. 'From heir to spare to no longer needed there,' as people put it when they thought he couldn't hear them.

"Not quite."

Soft yellow light bloomed suddenly in the darkness as three pale orbs rose from the stranger's left hand. Dia recognized them as 'the stars,' a minor gift of cosmic power, though useful within its limits. Against the rain and the night three glowing orbs did little to light the aviary, but it did illuminate the stranger's face and the golden eyes which watched Dia with all the cunning consideration of a hunting fox.

"Then what?" Dia held his face in the neutral expressionless mask it had taken him so many years to perfect, acknowledging nothing, revealing nothing.

"Three favors." The man's lips curved in a fox's smile.

Dia studied him consideringly. "Name them."

The Fox shook his head. "Oh no, not like that."

Dia's eyes widened, his whole body stiffening as he realized what the Fox actually meant. Feeling his tension, Frost shifted a little on Dia's arm, her talons digging in with every movement. Dia ignored the discomfort, focusing all of his attention on the Fox.

"You want a blank note."

The Fox nodded and raised three of the fingers of his right hand.

"Three favors to be named later. Whatever I want, whenever I want them."

Dia pursed his lips. It was hardly the sort of deal he wanted to agree to. After so many years spent amassing little favors and debts that he could call in when needed, he knew *exactly* how dangerous such an agreement was. But in his current position what choice did he have? If the queen found out he knew... No, he couldn't take that risk, no matter what he had to promise.

"On one condition."

"Are you in a position to make conditions?" Amusement glinted in the Fox's eyes. Dia stared calmly back.

"Am I?" He asked the question lightly, calmly even, because threats always held more strength when made calmly. He didn't reach for the dagger at his waist or say anything to make the threat more obvious because the more subtle the threat, the less obvious its emptiness.

If the Fox were to die, then that would be the end of it: no favors owed, no secrets revealed. Yet Dia knew already that the Fox would leave the aviary safely. He'd never killed anyone—and the thought of taking a life turned the prince's heart to ice and panic—but that wasn't the reason. It was simply the mismatch in their abilities. Dia had trained from childhood in self-defense and he had worked hard at his lessons. Bare handed or with a dagger Dia was sure that if the Fox tried to take his life Dia could throw him off and escape. But escape was one thing and murder was another. Unlike the king's other children, Dia had none of the combat training meant for a battlefield commander meanwhile the Fox was dressed in the uniform of a guard. Unless the uniform was stolen that made him no less than a trained killer.

Against those odds the prince would be a fool to take that kind of chance, but unlike his status in the court, Dia's lack of training and the reasons behind it were not commonly known. He'd worked hard to keep that particular vulnerability as secret as he could and so, as long as the Fox had not somehow learned of it, the threat should mean something to him.

The Fox was quiet for a few seconds, seeming to think it through, then he asked, "What's your condition?"

Outwardly Dia's expression didn't change but inwardly he let out a sigh of relief.

"Tell me your name."

The Fox was quiet for a long moment, studying Dia, his golden eyes considering. Above them rain drummed on the roof of the aviary. All around them in the darkness birds shifted in nests and on perches, their wings rustling. In the highest tower of the Crown the great clock struck ten, the chime of its voice ringing through the night.

"It's Calix."

THE NEXT MORNING Dia sent his half-sibling Evren to ask one of the watch captains what she knew about a guard by the name of Calix. It was hardly a subtle approach but Dia didn't think there was any need for subtlety. Only a fool would have given Dia his name and not expected an investigation to follow, considering how quickly Calix had pieced together Dia's situation and turned it to his advantage, the Fox was anything but a fool.

Ordinarily Dia would have gone himself to speak with the watch captain if only for the chance to continue building their relationship. Reeva Mellory was a smart capable office and Dia had been working hard to foster both her talents and her loyalty, giving her little suggestions and pieces of information to pass off as her own so that she could impress her superiors. Today however, going himself wasn't an option—not with the way his head spun as his body extracted its price for the previous day's escape and not with the new threat which hung above him, a clock ticking down to its inevitable end. Before last night, before the queen's garden, Dia hadn't even known the clock was there and now its hands were already nearing midnight. And when they struck, when the time was up...

He would be dead.

CHAPTER 3
BLOOD PRICE

ar Mel, capital of the kingdom of H'arn, was built in a series of concentric rings. The outermost and largest was the People's City, a bustle of winding streets, crowds and markets, where older two- and three- and four-story houses towered over modern single story buildings with their rooves of gray or orange slate which were beginning to spring up in wealthier districts. The second circle was the Palace City. Richer and more ornamented as it was, only a handful of the old multi-story buildings remained within its walls, but in many other ways the Palace City looked no different than the People's City, so filled was it with guards and servants, nobles, officials, craftsmen, soldiers, grooms, smiths, and all the other people needed in the running of a nation constantly at war.

The third ring was far smaller than the other two. The Crown stood at the very heart of Tar Mel, its three great towers rising high above even the outer wall of the people's city. Each was wrought of white marble and topped with a pointed roof which sheltered a watch platform. In the center-most of the three towers was set the great clock which chimed each half hour for all of Tar Mel to hear. Below the three towers lay the vast expanse of the hall of Adjra, named for the goddess-queen of battles, where all of the realm's great audiences and ceremonies were held. Stretching out from either side of the Crown's three towers and the hall beneath them, was a crenelated guard wall which ran in a circle from either side of the towers until they met behind it, forming the 'band' of the Crown. Inside those walls stood the residences and gardens of the royal family of H'arn.

All except Dia's.

He, his mother and half siblings lived on one edge of the Palace City, the house and its placement nice enough to honor Lady Derya's status as a member of the ruling family of Sinotalya, a merchant city in H'arn's north, without ever acknowledging Dia's own status. Yet it wasn't something Dia resented. If anything he was grateful for it, for the privacy made keeping his secret that much easier.

Dia cut through the streets of the Palace City with the ease of a lifetime's worth of familiarity, his long hair braided and tucked securely beneath a gray cap to conceal his identity. His light brown skin and half-Talyian features were unusual in the Palace City but not extraordinary enough to cause comment. His hair however...

"Birth was stressful for him." That was what the midwife told his mother. Whether that was true or whether the lack of pigment in his hair had more to do with the same assertion of his father's genetics that had also given him his pale eyes, Dia didn't know but whatever the reason, his hair had been nothing but silvery gray from the day he was born. It was why, once his hood was gone, both Calix and the guards from the night before had been able to identify him at a glance and the reason that, unless he had been summoned to the Crown in some official capacity, Dia rarely left home without either a hood or a hat.

By day the city which had been so quiet the night before had come alive with noise and bustle. Today he could sense a little extra tension in the air, the solders walking a little faster, the servants and craftsman talking more quickly. The war with Estron, H'arn's old and bitter enemy, had been at a standstill for fully half a season, and now the rumor was spreading that the king was planning some new great push that would break the stalemate. More evidence of the city's preparation for battle came as Dia passed the entrance to Crafters' Row and saw the smoke rising over the ally. The king had instructed his craftsmen to focus all their attention on building mounts and rotating platforms for the fire-powder weapons the mechanists of the Yingtian Dutchie were producing for him. On a different day Dia might have gone down the Row to watch the crafts masters at work and learn what he could from them, but even if he hadn't had other things to worry about, today wasn't one of the good days and so he couldn't take the risk. For a few moments Dia paused, leaning against the wall of a nearby building to steady himself, and then he continued on. His goal wasn't much farther, and that was a good thing.

Just a little ways past Crafter's Row Dia came to one of the few two-story buildings left in the Palace City, the Temple of Cylbra, king of the wind, god of sky and birds and clear sight. Dia rarely went inside the temple but just being around it always calmed his mind, clearing some of the dizzy vagueness from it, leading Dia to guess that some of the sky god's power must hang in the air around his place of worship. As he felt the familiar presence of Cylbra wash over him, Dia let out a soft sigh of relief and, walking faster now, passed around the back of the temple and into the space between building and city wall. The hollow was one of the Palace City's hidden gems, a beautiful memorial garden in the Zheng style to honor the late queen Su Yin, mother of crown princess Emira, who had been a follower of Cylbra. Yet Emira rarely came to the hollow and no one else seemed to remember its existence, so with the power of Cylbra so close beside it, Dia found the hollow the perfect place to think. And think he needed to. Desperately.

Settled on the ground beneath the red leafed canopy of his usual tree Dia closed his eyes for a moment, basking in the feeling of Cylbra's power as it cleared the fog from his mind and sharpening his awareness. This was why he dragged himself out here, even on the difficult days when his mind hazed and his body screamed for bed The god's power gave him back the clarity of thought that he otherwise lost to the dizzying dark.

Dia gave himself only a moment to enjoy the sensation then he opened his eyes, pulled the record book from his satchel, and stared at it. The book was written in cypher and contained everything: every favor he had given, every bit of information he had ever or could ever leverage, every single name of every single person who might owe him even the slightest bit of aid. Having it all written down was dangerous, he knew that, but it was too much for even him to carry unscrambled in his own head and so, the cypher. He had been fifteen when he'd devised it and in the six years since he had become so familiar with its scribbled numbers that he could read them like a second language. Now he stared at those years of scrawled notes, desperately flipping through page after page as he searched for something, anything, any thread that he could pull which might help him stay in the game just a little longer, survive just a little longer.

There was nothing.

Of course there wasn't.

None of the lower level officials or captains or servants, or even the few nobles who owed him favors would ever be able to do anything to stand against the queen. How could they? No, a few favors weren't going to solve anything this time. He needed to stop panicking. He needed to think. Dia took a deep breath, closed the record book, and then his eyes. This was different then the small schemes and petty power plays he had involved himself in before. This was bigger—so much bigger—and that changed the rules, changed the players. It ruled out all of Dia's usual helpers, those little favors he'd given and fostered to earn himself some capital with the lower levels of the court, but even while it ruled them out ...It ruled someone else in, didn't it? Dia's father, King Harlin Amarth Demiter. As it was, he couldn't approach the king with this, but if Dia could bring him evidence, if Dia could put proof behind his words, then...

Dia's eyes flicked open and again he flipped through the pages, searching, not for an idea this time, but for an ally. He needed evidence, which meant that he needed to slip into the queen's chambers and search them, then slip into the chambers of her allies and search there as well. Only he couldn't. Not today. Not on a bad day. Maybe tomorrow would be better, or maybe it would take a week until his mind cleared and his body responded properly again, and with every hour that passed the clock ticked closer to midnight. He didn't know how long he had and he couldn't afford to wait. That meant he needed someone to act for him, someone he could trust enough to ask them to risk their life slipping into the queen's quarters and know that they would not betray him, someone who he could tell the truth of his own weakness and the reason why he could not undertake this task himself.

Frantically Dia flicked through page after page of his journal, searching for possibilities, and came up with no one. His step cousin Jamal would have done it, but Jamal was stationed down at the Estron border, on the other side of the Sky Stone mountains, a full two weeks' ride away. Fast and unhindered by geography as they were, one of Dia's falcons could reach him in just a couple of days. But even if Jamal found a way to extract himself from his command and ride immediately for Tar Mel he would likely only arrive in time to witness Dia's funeral. No, he needed someone else, someone already within the capital, someone...

"There you are, Prince."

Dia stiffened, head snapping up to stare at the man standing above him.

It was Calix.

The Fox was out of uniform today, dressed in dark brown trousers and heeled boots which added a couple of inches to his height. His open necked red tunic should have clashed horribly with the orange of his hair but somehow managed to work with it instead, only increasing his resemblance to the canine Dia had privately nicknamed him for.

"How did you find me here?"

The Fox ignored the question, his eyes moving with interest to the book in the prince's hand. Dia's own eyes narrowed as he snapped it shut.

"Have you been following me?"

Calix just shrugged. "What do you think?"

I think I might have to figure out how to remove you after all.

"What do you want?" Dia countered, forcing his body to relax and his expression to drop back into neutrality.

The Fox held up one slim finger and as his hand moved the sleeve of his tunic fell back to reveal a tattoo, black against the pale skin of his wrist. Eleven stars with lines branching between them to connect the constellation. Five stars formed a head with pointed ears, the other six marking out a curving back, the tips of front paws and the curl of a bushy tail. A sitting fox, how fitting. Yet Dia highly doubted the tattoo had anything to do with the orange hair or clever tongue which had connected Calix to the animal in his mind, for he recognized this constellation. It was the mark of the Star Fox, the god of peace, one of the six great gods of the Hexium, said to be the leaders of the divine realm. Was Calix a follower of the Star Fox? Or did the tattoo hold a different meaning? Dia had heard that recently, on the northeastern continent, tattoos of the Hexium's various star signs were being used as shorthand for various genders. In the last couple of years the practice had even begun to spread on their own continent. Dia was about to ask which of the two was the reason for the tattoo but Calix spoke before he could.

"I'm here for my first favor."

Dia's eyes narrowed. "What do you want?"

Calix eyed him for a moment then the corners of his lips curved in a sly smile.

"I want to know what you learned in the queen's garden last night."

Dia stiffened, unable to hide his shock. Whatever he had expected the Fox to ask for it wasn't this. A flurry of thoughts raced through the prince's mind, his knuckles turning white where they clutched his notebook. Why would Calix want to know? Was he working for the queen after all? Trying to find out how much he knew? No, that didn't make sense. Even if the queen wanted to pull off such an elaborate trap the timeline didn't work. To catch Dia before he could fall off the roof Calix would have had to leave the queen's garden no later than the other guards who had chased after him the instant he slipped in his descent from the tree he'd been perched in. There would have been no time for the queen to come up with such a plot and send another after him. No, the Fox was acting on his own initiative, which actually begged another question...

"Well?" Calix asked.

"How do you know I was in the queen's garden?" Dia asked the question partly out of interest and partly to buy time to think.

Calix eyed him thoughtfully and for a moment Dia thought he wouldn't answer but then the Fox dropped down into the grass to seat himself cross legged, his back against a large decorative rock.

"You left the garden door propped open. I found it and decided to hang around and find out who was sneaking into the queen's garden."

Dia started at that and he was about to ask what a royal guard had been doing checking the queen's garden door anyway but the words died on his lips as things began to add up. Dia had followed servant's rumors into the queen's garden that night. He'd thought he was the only one in the court who actually bothered to make friends and contacts out of the servants. Clearly he'd been wrong. Calix must have followed the same rumors he had, only when he'd arrived at the garden Calix had found that someone had beaten him to the mark. Not wanting to risk getting caught by the competition, Calix had hidden and waited to find out who had gotten there first then looked for a way to get the information out of Dia. Now the only question was why. Had Calix thought to blackmail the queen for his own benefit or, more likely, was he working for one of the court's other factions?

"Hey prince, you can't just stare into the distance until I go away you know."

Dia started. Calix's words jerking him back into reality.

"This isn't information you want." Whoever Calix was working for or even if he was driven purely by his own self-interest he deserved that warning at least.

The Fox's eyes narrowed. "That dangerous, is it? Now I just want to know even more."

Dia drummed his fingers on the cover of the notebook. His first instinct was to find some way to deflect, keeping the secret close as he kept all of his secrets. And yet... if he didn't tell then Calix might hand him over to the queen. He could lie of course, come up with some false scandal to pass off as what he'd heard. He could claim that his father the king had taken a secret mistress and that there were rumors of another bastard or that the queen's eldest daughter had a secret illness or something like that.

And yet...

Dia considered Calix again. A royal guard could go almost anywhere in the Palace City unquestioned, and this particular royal guard clearly knew a thing or two about lying and about sneaking into the few places that his uniform wouldn't take him.

"After this, I will still owe you two favors won't I?"
"You will."
Dia sat up a bit straighter, eyes meeting Calix's.
"I can't grant you favors if I'm dead."
The Fox's eyes narrowed farther. "No, you can't..." A

small smile curved the corners of his lips. "Alright, tell me. How will this secret be the death of me."

Dia's eyes flicked left and right. He knew they were alone but he had to be sure. He'd already missed Calix following him, probably due to the fog in his own head, but here, in this garden touched by Cylbra's power, his mind was clear and if he played this right...

"I am to be framed for murder and executed for it."

Calix's eyes widened at that. Whatever he had expected it clearly wasn't this.

"Whose murder?"

"Crown Princess Emira."

The Fox sucked in a breath. "So the queen wants her daughter to be heir by any means."

"No." Dia corrected him, his voice calm in a way that belied the racing of his heart. "The queen is plotting a coup."

CHAPTER 4
THE FIRST FAVOR

Calix stiffened, shock clearly written across his face, his hand twitching reflexively in the direction of his dagger before he caught himself and stilled again, eyes fixed on Dia.

"Explain."

There was a new intensity in his voice, a falling away of the light, careless quality which had marked it till that point. Dia couldn't blame him. He hadn't exactly been calm when he'd learned the truth either. In fact, it had been that shock which lead him to slip his way back down the tree in the queen's garden, causing the sounds that had nearly gotten him caught.

"What do you know about the Warlord of the West?"

"Oh..." Calix let the word out on a soft breath and Dia nodded.

"Princess Castela turns sixteen next season doesn't she?"

Dia nodded again. Princess Castela, the elder of Queen Reanun's two children, was indeed a season away from her sixteenth birthday, the day she would become eligible to take the throne. Until then, should she become heir and the king die, she would need a regent. That was where the Warlord of the West came in. Governor Cimaura Korvin had earned her title through bloody efficiency. She was said to be an ambitious, ruthless woman on and off of the battlefield, and she was also the queen's elder sister. In fact, it was in hopes of controlling her ambition and gaining control of her army that King Harlin had married Cimaura's younger sister to begin with. Yet it seemed now to have done the opposite. If Emira was murdered and Dia executed for that murder, the king would naturally name Castela as heir. Once she was heir if anything were to happen to the king before Castela reached her sixteenth year, who better to act as regent than a respected warlord like Cimaura? And if the regent never actually stood aside for her niece... Well Dia was sure she and her sister would come up with a nice marriage alliance for Castela or something of the sort.

"Trickster," Calix cursed under his breath, his fingers beginning to drum against the ground. "Gates take the Adjra-cursed lot of them." He scooped up a fallen twig and threw it in the direction of the Palace City wall.

Dia's eyes narrowed slightly. He had expected shock and horror or maybe disbelief and denial but this was neither, this was anger, frustration, resentment, and that was... That was interesting. It could've been simple patriotism of course, but Dia didn't think so. There was no indignation in Calix's tone, none of the self-righteous rage which would have suggested his anger to be a product of loyalty to king and country. No, this was something else, and Dia filed it away to consider later.

"What's your plan?" Calix asked the question with an abrupt sharpness which made the prince start. The Fox was looking at him through narrowed golden eyes, the anger he had heard earlier still reflected in their depths.

"Recruiting you."

This time it was Calix's turn to start, his eyes widening as he rocked back until his shoulders collided with the boulder behind him.

Dia had to work hard to suppress a small smile at that. In all of their brief acquaintance he had never seen his blackmailer so unbalanced and it felt like a bit of a triumph. Dia had considered several different ways to approach his request for assistance but after seeing the anger flickering so clear in Calix's eyes he'd suspected the straightforward approach might capitalize on the emotion and turn it to his advantage. Now to see if he had been right…

"Explain."

"I need help. I don't want to tell more people about this then I have to since everyone who knows is one more person in danger or one more person who could sell me out to the queen, and it's as I said before. I can't grant you favors if I'm dead." Dia spoke plainly, his eyes locked on the Fox's face, searching it for the first hint of a reaction.

For his part Calix stared back, leaning forward as he studied Dia, his eyes narrowing in consideration. At last he asked. "What *exactly* do you need this helper to do?"

Dia sucked in a breath. This was the hard part. How to explain this without revealing his secret… "If I bring this to the king then that will be the end of it, but I can't do so without proof. I need someone to sneak into the queen's quarters and into the quarters of her allies to search for evidence of what I overheard."

Calix arched an eyebrow at him. "Why not go yourself?"

Dia did his best not to flinch at the question. "Guards

can move around the Crown more freely than a disinherited prince."

"Is that it or are you too much of a Demiter to risk your own neck?" The barb was swift and filled with a sudden bitter fury that Dia did not expect.

"It isn't like that!" He snapped, starting upward in anger only to sway, the world momentarily blacking out as his hand sought desperately for the tree behind him and he leaned back against it, head coming to rest against the bark.

Instantly Calix was on his feet as well, stepping toward Dia who quickly raised his free hand to ward him off. Calix stilled, his eyes narrowing.

"What is it?"

"It's nothing. I just stood up too fast."

They glared at each other for a moment then Calix abruptly spun on his heal. For a moment Dia feared that he was just going to walk away, but the Fox only began pacing back and forth between his rock and an ornamental fish pond a few feet away. Dia watched him in silence, using the reprieve to slide back down the trunk of the tree and reach into the same shoulder bag he'd been carrying his book of notes in. From its depths he pulled out a flask, unscrewed the lid, and took a long drink. The contents were salty on his tongue but he drank them down anyway, the ginger syrup his half sibling brewed for the mixture cutting the worst of the flavor.

"Diamond Havoran Demiter."

Dia's head jerked up to find that Calix had stopped his pacing just in front of him. The Fox's gaze was considering as he rolled the prince's name across his tongue, something about the way he said it sparking an odd sort of tension in Dia.

"The disinherited first heir to the throne, too much of a

reclusive scholar to bother himself with politics." The Fox had clearly gotten himself back under control because the teasing note was back in his voice. "At least that's what everyone says of you. But it's not true is it?"

Dia stiffened, his heart pounding and dread coiling in his stomach like one of Princess Emira's pet serpents. "What do you mean?" Somehow he managed to keep his voice level despite the panic building in his chest.

A smile curved the corners of Calix's mouth. "Why would a reclusive bookworm with no political ambitions be sneaking into the queen's garden in the middle of a rainy night to overhear her secret counsel? It turned out to have to do with you, but you had no way of knowing that. Just the fact that you knew about the meeting to begin with suggests a network of informants and allies among the servants, which doesn't make sense at all for someone not interested in politics. So perhaps you are a secret politician. But then where is your faction? The court allies you could go to with this? Maybe you don't have any. Maybe you've never let anyone get close enough to form a real alliance or maybe you just can't risk them asking you the same question I did. Either way it comes to the same thing doesn't it?"

"Does it?" Dia's voice at last slipped the bounds of his carefully wrought control. He could hear the hoarseness in it, hear the way it shook ever so slightly, betraying him just the way his body always did.

Calix stepped closer until he was standing just above Dia. "You nearly fell when you stood up in the aviary. The same thing happened just now. You have a reputation as a recluse—even when you have an explicit assignment from the king you have a tendency to disappear—and I'd bet the trickster themself that flask doesn't have alcohol in it. You're sick, aren't you Demiter?"

"I'm not!" The denial slipped from Dia's lips, quick and desperate and hardly convincing. He couldn't help it, not with the panic roaring in his ears with every beat of his racing treacherous heart. All these years. All these years keeping himself hidden, keeping out of the public eye, never traveling, never committing to anything he couldn't find a way to excuse himself from, the isolation, the bribes to the doctors, all of it, and now...

Calix crossed his arms. "Really?"

Dia's hand tightened around the flask until his knuckles paled. He balled his other hand into a fist, desperate to hide the way it was shaking. "I told you I'm not. I just don't like being around people. That's all. All I did was stumble twice and you're really going to make this much out of it?"

His voice came out steadier this time, more convincing, but he wasn't sure it mattered. The damage was probably already done.

"Is it fatal?" There was no mockery to Calix's tone when he asked the question but no sympathy in it either. His expression had turned considering in a way that sent a chill down Dia's spine.

"I told you, I'm not sick."

"Oh really?" Calix arched an eyebrow at him, the mockery returning. "Then get up and walk out of here. Go on." Calix gestured to the path out of the garden. "Do it."

Dia glared up at him, his mind racing in time with his heartbeat. He could try, could get up slowly, walk away. He was good at hiding the signs, good at moving slowly enough that he could keep his shoulders straight and his gait even, good at digging his nails into his palms hard enough that the pain would keep him conscious, keep him moving, but that was when deceiving people who didn't know, people who weren't looking for the signs. If Dia tried that now with Calix would he be able to pull it off or would it be obvious the moment he carefully levered himself off of the ground? Did it even matter? Calix was already convinced Dia was sick and with a sinking feeling Dia realized there was nothing he could do to destroy that conviction.

The prince must have hesitated for too long because a triumphant smile curved the corners of Calix's lips. "There. Now you might as well stop this and tell me."

Dia gritted his teeth. It was one thing to have the Fox blackmailing him about the queen and her plots, one annoying frustrating thing, but Dia had already figured out how to spin that to his advantage. This though...This was so much bigger. Even if Dia figured out how to survive the queens plot's this could still destroy him, a threat which had no end. If Calix was merely working for himself, a clever man taking advantage of the situation, then that could be managed. If he wasn't though, if he was, as Dia suspected, in the service of one of the court's other factions, then whoever he was working for would have the ability to destroy Dia at any moment and the prince wouldn't even know who they were.

"I haven't kept my secrets for this long just to give them to you."

"How long is 'this long?'"

"I'm not going to answer your questions."

Calix shrugged. "Then I'm not going to help you."

Dia started at that but then his eyes narrowed. "You're going to let the queen kill the heir to the throne *and* the king just to spite me?"

Calix looked steadily back. "I'm not going to work with someone who has a weakness they won't explain."

They glared at each other for a moment, Dia clenching

and unclenching his fist. The words were reasonable and yet...

"Are you blackmailing me for your own advancement or are you working for someone?"

Calix's eyes narrowed. "Trying to figure out how easy it will be to silence me, Demiter?"

"Trying to figure out who's after my secrets."

Calix considered him for a moment, some emotion Dia couldn't catch flickering behind his eyes, and when he spoke again his tone had softened. "I won't tell anyone."

"Oh really?" Dia raised a skeptical eyebrow at him."

Calix nodded, his eyes flicking away from Dia to study the tree behind him and the garden all around them. "You don't have any reason to trust my word but I'll give it to you anyway for whatever that's worth."

Dia stared at him for a long moment, every instinct in him screaming not to trust this, to keep the secret which he had spent so much of his life protecting clutched to his chest till his dying breath, and yet... And yet that dying breath was coming soon wasn't it? Depending how quickly the queen put her own plan into action, Dia could be imprisoned for murder by the end of the week, dead in another week. He needed help, needed allies. Much as he hated to admit it, he needed Calix.

"Fourteen."

"What?" The Fox's eyes snapped back to Dia's face.

"Fourteen years. That's how long I've been hiding this." He let out a long breath, leaning back against the tree. "It's called the Wrong Blood Disease."

Calix blinked then shook his head. "I haven't heard of it." All the mockery and triumph was gone from his voice, leaving it curious and a little bit kind, a kindness Dia in no way trusted.

"I'm not surprised. It isn't well known."

The Fox eyed him for a moment then retreated to his rock and perched on top of it.

"So it's a blood disease?"

Dia shook his head. "They used to think it was but it isn't." He took a deep breath and closed his eyes. He might as well do this properly, after all it wasn't as though the Fox couldn't simply borrow a medical text from the library. He opened his eyes. "You know how every time your heart beats it pushes the blood back up your body against gravity?"

Calix nodded.

"Well mine doesn't always."

Calix started at that. "Why not?"

Dia shook his head. "No one knows. They used to think it was a problem with the blood, maybe that the blood was too thick or something, hence the name Wrong Blood, but my blood isn't any different from anyone else's. Then they thought it was a heart problem but they can't find anything wrong with my heart either. To answer your question, no, it isn't fatal. But without knowing the cause it isn't curable either. All they can do is treat the symptoms."

"Which are?"

"On good days? Nothing. Everything is normal. On bad days..." Dia looked away, eyes dropping to his flask. "When I'm vertical there isn't enough blood reaching my brain. My mind can get foggy, it's hard to think, harder the longer I stand or even sit. I get spinny, lightheaded, and if I stay upright too long or get up too quickly I'll pass out or collapse."

Dia's eyes darted back to the Fox, shoulders tensing against the pity or triumph he expected to see in his blackmailer's eyes. But the Fox's expression was only thoughtful and he simply nodded, his eyes again moving away from Dia, this time in the direction of the Temple of Cylbra. He said nothing. Unsure what else to do, Dia uncorked his flask and took another drink, hoping it would fortify him against whatever was to come.

He was recorking the flask when Calix finally spoke.

"Alright."

Dia looked up at him, tension radiating through his body. "Alright what?"

Calix stood, lips curving slightly as he stepped forward and extended a hand to Dia. "I'm going to help you home, if you'll let me, and then it seems I have some royal rooms to break into."

CHAPTER 5

THE SOLDIER

"Crimson Age: A term coined around the year 50 of the new "Post Cataclysm" (PC) calendar. It describes the state of affairs in our world beginning with our defeat in the Dragons' War and the closing of the world gates and continues until this very day (Spring 200PC). The term comes from the tides of blood which have washed our world since nations that so long relied on inter-world trade and conquest as the backbone of their economies suddenly found themselves permanently cut off from every world but our own. Left with the finite resources of our own three continents and myriad islands, and still militarized after years of fighting in the Dragons' War, our largest nations sought land and resources in the only way that made sense to them. They turned on each other. Now 200 years deep into the crimson age the world still runs red and I doubt that it will ever end."

-From the writings of Prince Diamond Havoran Demiter

EVREN WAS WAITING on the bench outside their house when he got home. They had a book in their lap and were flicking

✦ 38 ✦

through the pages, but Dia wasn't fooled. He knew they had been waiting, and it made his heart squeeze a little in mingled guilt and gratitude just as it always did. At fourteen Evren was the elder of his two half siblings. Technically he had five siblings, two by his mother and three by his father, but Dia barely knew his royal siblings, distant figures he sometimes crossed paths with around the court, without any trust or bond between them. Evren and Ruslan though? They were his—siblings of his heart as well as of his blood, the ones who he had grown up with, looked after and cared for, the ones who now took it upon themselves, young as they were, to look after him during their mother's absences.

Sure enough, Evren's eyes flicked upward from the book the instant Dia approached the house only for them to stiffen, their carefully casual glance turning to alarmed stare as they registered the red-haired man with his arm around Dia's waist. The prince could hardly blame them. When Calix had extended his hand to Dia in the garden, the prince had studied it warily for nearly a minute before grudgingly taking it and allowing himself to be pulled to his feet. It wasn't that Dia minded being helped in principle. Needing something or someone to lean on sometimes was simply one of the realities of his life and he had long since gotten used to it. Through most of his teen years Ozan, his mother's late husband, had been the one supporting him, helping him around the house or into the garden on bad days just as he had taught Dia self-defense on good ones. But Ozan had been dead for five years now and there had been few people to help him since.

His mother did sometimes, as did Hazan, their cook who had first come to Tar Mel with his mother two and a half decades earlier and who, in her absolute loyalty to

Lady Derya, was the only person outside of the family and the doctors permitted to know of Dia's condition. Yet Dia did his best not to ask for their help. He saw the strain his health and the secrecy that surrounded it put on both women and didn't want to worry them further. That was why, ever since Ozan's death, he had done his best to manage on his own even on the worst days, digging his nails into his palms and doing everything he could to hide his struggle to stand. He wasn't sure if he fooled them, but the one person he knew he had never managed to fool was Evren. After their father's death Evren had gone quiet and in that silence they seemed to have become more observant, seeing everything, even what Dia wanted to hide. They were the one who had noticed the way his lips pursed when he drank the salty medicine and had started experimenting with syrups of ginger root and lavender to cut the flavor. They were the one who seemed to have decided it was their job to watch over Dia in their mother's absence. Whether it was something they had come to on their own or whether their mother had put them up to it Dia wasn't sure and he wasn't sure he wanted to know.

"Dia, is everything alright?" Evren slid from their bench and approached him and the Fox, their dark gray eyes flicking warily from their brother to the stranger and back again.

"Everything's fine." Dia gave them a weak smile. When he'd finally accepted Calix's hand it had only been to help him stand. He had pulled away afterward, saying that he was fine to do the rest on his own. Calix hadn't argued but as they left the garden and walked farther and farther from the temple and Cylbra's influence, Dia's steps had begun to lag, his head lowering and his stride becoming uneven as he bit down on his lip, trying to ignore the black spots dancing in the corners of his eyes. Finally, after the third time Dia stumbled against a wall, Calix had offered his help again and this time the prince had accepted, allowing the Fox to wrap an arm around his waist while the prince rested his weight against Calix's shoulder. In his heeled boots, the Fox was as tall as Dia and the support, and the fact Dia no longer had to concentrate on not walking into anyone, helped. He had expected a mocking comment or a smirk when he finally gave in but he received neither, Calix remaining quiet for the rest of the walk. Much as Dia was furious with the Fox he had to admit to himself, he was also a little bit grateful.

Evren's eyes lingered skeptically on Dia but they said nothing aloud, only looked for a moment then turned and went quickly to the door, pulling it open so that Calix could help the prince inside. The entrance hall was warmly lit, with sun pouring in through the windows and reflecting off of the pattern of the blue and green tiles set into the walls in the Talyian style. As soon as they were inside Dia pulled away from Calix and dropped gratefully onto the ornately carved wooden bench beside the door. The pressure in his head seemed to lessen instantly. It wasn't gone by a long shot but merely the act of no longer being on his feet was enough to push back the dizzy blackness which had been trying to claim him their entire walk home. Still, it wasn't completely gone and wouldn't be until he could lie still and rest. His bed—oh how he wanted his bed. Dia let out a long breath and looked up then started as the first thing he saw was a pair of golden eyes studying him. For a moment the sheer relief of no longer being fully vertical had driven all thoughts of the Fox from his mind and now Dia struggled to pull them back into order so that he could deal with his unwanted guest. Should he thank the man? Calix had supported him most of the way from Cylbra's temple after all, yet that had only happened because the Fox had blackmailed and pressured him into revealing one of his deepest and most dangerous secrets, putting him permanently at the other man's mercy. How could that be worthy of thanks?

Before Dia could decide what to do he was saved by the sound of racing footsteps followed by a boy's head poking around the doorway. "Dia! You're back! Smoke just flew in half an hour ago! I saw her land in the aviary! I bet she has a letter from mother! We should..." The boy broke off abruptly, blinked rapidly, then drew himself up, as though finally noticing the stranger in the room. At age ten, Ruslan only came up to Calix's shoulder, so at the sight of him trying to stand tall and imposing Dia had to work hard to hide the amused twitching of his lips.

"Who are you?" Ruslan asked the question with all the bluntness of a hammer and Dia saw Evren wince.

Calix's lips twitched. "That's a question you should ask your brother."

Ruslan and Evren's eyes both flicked to Dia who uttered a mental curse before plastering a smile on his lips and fixing his eyes on Ruslan. "This is Calix. He's a friend." The word friend tasted wrong on his tongue but what else could he say? As he spoke the Fox's name he was careful to keep his gaze off of Evren, but from the corner of his eye he saw them stiffen slightly, their eyes widening as they recognized the man standing in their front hall as the one Dia had sent them to investigate. Had it been Ruslan who had delivered his request to the guard captain Dia would have looked for some way around saying Calix's name but he trusted Evren not to make a scene and, sure enough, they made not a sound. What a difference four years and the memory of their father's death could make. Ruslan had been only five when Ozan died, old enough to grieve certainly, but far too young to know anything of the true circumstances behind his death or to learn the same lessons from it that Dia and Evren had.

Not that Evren knew the full truth either, but the ways they had changed in the season following the funeral told Dia they must have figured out some part of it. How much exactly they knew, however, Dia wasn't sure. He had always been too scared to ask.

Even Ruslan seemed to have picked up some subtlety from growing up in court however, because instead of pointing out that Dia didn't have friends, couldn't have friends, he simply gave Calix a considering look and asked, "Are you staying?"

Calix shook his head. "I have an errand to run for your brother."

At that Dia's eyes snapped back to the Fox. "We should talk more before you run the errand." *We should come up with a plan before you attempt to sneak into the queen's chamber's.*

"No need." Calix turned back to him, a mischievous grin curving the corners of his lips, "I have my ways."

Dia's eyes narrowed. "Such as?"

"Nothing you need to worry about, Demiter. You just rest and I'll be back with what we agreed on." Calix waived a casual hand in Dia's direction, turned on his heel, and, just like that, he slipped past Evren and vanished out the door.

～

HOURS LATER, as sunset's light slanted through the ornately cut windows, Dia leaned back against the pillows of his bed and picked up the paper Evren had silently left on his bedside table next to yet another glass of salty medicine. This time they'd cut the medicine with the juice of the red spring berries that they tended in their garden. The paper was in their handwriting but the words were not theirs. They were from the book of personnel records which held the details of every member of the royal guard. Captain Mellory must have allowed Evren to copy it. Dia would need to find a way to do her another favor soon to thank her. The name at the top of the page was 'Calix Acalion.'

Besides basic information such as his age (19) and his height (5'9") there wasn't much written on the paper. Calix had been born on the outskirts of Car Culond a small but well-fortified city on the much contested border with the kingdom of Estron, H'arn's long time enemy. At fourteen he had begun training to join the city guard and, at sixteen, once he had reached his adulthood, he had done exactly that. There he had been assigned to guard the part of the border near his home village and had caught the eye of Salvor Moston, the reclusive old Governor who ruled over Car Culond and the land surrounding it. It had been the recommendation letter sealed with the Moston family crest which, along with his skills, had earned Calix a place in the royal guard when he came to Tar Mel only a quarter of a year earlier. Beyond that there was a commendation for catching a thief in the Palace City, another one for catching a spy from Palia, and that was it.

Dia frowned at the paper. He hadn't expected Calix to be so new to Tar Mel and that troubled him. A season wasn't likely to be enough time to ingratiate himself to any of the court's various political factions which might have decided to use him to spy on the queen. It was possible that he had done some major service for one of them which had been kept out of his file or that he really was an opportunist working on his own or... Dia tapped his fingers against the bedside table trying to recall everything he knew about Governor Moston. There wasn't much. The old man was said to be a recluse and hadn't traveled to Tar Mel within Dia's lifetime. As far as the prince knew Moston didn't have any ties to Tar Melion politics though he supposed it was always possible. ... Or possible that there was an ambitious retainer or grandchild hiding somewhere in Moston's shadow.

Dia pushed himself into a sitting position and was relieved to find that only a little of the earlier lightheadedness still clung around him. He pulled the pen and paper he always kept nearby toward himself and began to scribble a note, not in the complex code he had concocted for his journal but in a childish scrawl of lines and shapes, each one taking the place of a letter. It was far from uncrackable. Any code breaker worth the name could fill in Es and Is for the most often repeated letter shapes and unscramble the thing from there, but they would have to get ahold of the note first. Frost was as temperamental as she was well trained and the combination meant that anyone outside of Dia's immediate family who tried to take her letter from her was likely to lose a finger for their trouble. There was only one exception to that rule, only one other person Dia had trained the falcon to seek and trust. It was the same person who held the key to this particular code, having created this new alphabet with Dia when they were both children. His step-cousin Jamal, the only person Dia fully trusted outside of his immediate family and who by the trickster's blessing, was currently stationed at Car Culond, perfectly positioned to pay a visit to Lord Moston and uncover the secrets of Calix's past.

Once Ruslan ran off to the aviary with the letter there was nothing for Dia to do but lie back against his pillows and wait. He tried to read, first a report on unusual troop deployments that had arrived from Jamal three days earlier and then, when he couldn't get his mind to focus on untangling the meaning behind the strange withdrawals Jamal's commander had ordered, a book of epic poetry he had borrowed from the palace library. It was no use. The later the hour got the twitchier he became. 'I have my ways' Calix had said, yet what did he really mean by that? Was he referring to whatever servant contacts had led him to the queen's garden the night before? Was he relying on them to sneak him into their mistress's quarters now? Or did the Fox have some other trick up his sleeves? Something deceptive or crafty to match the nickname Dia had given him? Calix was certainly a clever man, but he was also an arrogant one and arrogant men could make mistakes. What if he had overestimated his abilities? What if he had trusted someone who sold him out to the queen after all? What if he was even now lying in chains somewhere in the dungeon below the Crown? How would Dia know? And what would he do if that was the case? Try to rescue him? Try to silence him before he could buy his safety with Dia's secrets?

...Or could it be that he was not in danger at all? That he had already betrayed Dia to the queen? Or that he had simply decided to stand back and do nothing while first Princess Emira then Dia died? How long should Dia wait to hear from him? When should he start trying to make other plans? What should he…

A quiet tapping on his window interrupted Dia's thoughts and when his head snapped up he found his gaze caught and held buy a pair of golden eyes on the other side of the glass. It was Calix.

Dia slipped from the bed and crossed the room quickly to undo the latch and push the window outward before standing back to let the Fox lift himself over the sill. As soon as Calix was inside Dia pulled the window shut and latched it again then turned back to his visitor to find the Fox studying him. After returning home Dia had traded his shirt and vest for an un-belted sleeveless tunic in faded turquoise and a pair of soft gray pants, but somehow he didn't feel that it was his informal clothing that Calix was looking at.

"Well?"

Calix's eyes roved over him again but all he said was. "You seem better."

Ah… That was it. After so many years of hiding his secret the comment coming from someone Dia barely new felt strange and wrong but he shrugged off both the feeling and the words. There were more important things to focus on.

"Are you going to tell me what you meant by 'I have my ways?'"

The Fox's lips curved slightly. "No."

Dia crossed his arms, feeling anger rising in him. After all the secrets Calix forced him to reveal…

"It's hard to come up with a plan if you won't tell me what assets we're working with."

"You don't need a plan. You need this." During his absence Calix had traded his tunic and brown trousers for the gold-buttoned black short coat and black trousers of the royal guard. The short coat was unfastened, revealing the white button-down shirt beneath and, as Dia watched, Calix slipped his hand inside the coat to where he must have cut a pocket into the lining. From it he pulled a single piece of paper and presented it to Dia with a mocking bow.

"Your Highness."

Gritting his teeth against his irritation Dia took the paper and unfolded it to reveal slanting handwriting and an entire page of numbers. "15-495 15-356 33-54..." His eyes narrowed. "Whose encrypted letter is this?"

Calix straightened, the mischievous satisfaction on his face only growing. "The queen's."

"What!" Dia started, then stared at him in utter shock. "You already broke into the queen's chambers and stole her correspondence just like that?"

"Copied, not stole," the Fox corrected, still sounding much too pleased with himself. "Once you've decrypted it I'll go back in steal the real one, but this way if it takes a while she won't notice it's gone."

A wave of unease crashed over Dia. That was too easy. That was far too easy. For Calix to pull off something like this on only a few hour's notice either he had friends among the queen's servants who had assisted him or this was some kind of fake, some kind of trap. He still doubted that the Fox was working for the queen—the timing simply didn't make sense—but that didn't mean he and Calix were necessarily on the same side. Still, with everything at stake and all the power the Fox now had over him, Dia would need to take the chance that this was real and act accordingly. He would just have to do so while watching for the double cross.

Turning away from Calix Dia crossed the room to his desk and seated himself, placing the paper in front of him.

"What do you know about this?"

Calix followed him to his desk and, without invitation, perched himself on one corner. "I found it locked in the queen's desk. The seal on the outside of the original had been broken but not destroyed. It belonged to the Warlord of the West.

Dia's eyes narrowed. "Then if we can crack it this is probably exactly the evidence we need." *Assuming it's real...*

The prince felt a sudden urge to glance at the man beside him to see if his face showed anything but he restrained himself, schooling his expression and hiding away his distrust. If this was a trap any show of skepticism might give away Dia's suspicions, and at the moment pretending that he didn't suspect was about the only advantage he had when it came to the Fox. And if it wasn't a trap, if Calix really did just have a friend or lover among the queen's household, someone in a position to help him steal this? Doing his best to block out the mingled unease and irritation he felt toward his uninvited guest, Dia bent over the message, studying it. During his years of encoding his own messages and writings Dia had spent as much time familiarizing himself with how to crack code as how to create it, trying to defeat himself with an endless series of exercises all geared to make his codes as hard to break as possible. Now he put those skills to work, calculating how many times each individual number or pair of numbers or set of numbers was written on the paper, then attempting to assign the most common letters or words to those which repeated most often, looking for patterns, for hints that what he was creating made some sort of sense. Somewhere in the back of his mind Dia could feel a slight lingering fog, a lightheadedness left over from the morning, but he had rested and he had drunk his medicine and it was possible now, seated and with a puzzle before him, to push the fog away and focus only on the work.

When the clock in the highest tower of the Crown rang out, marking the hour as two in the morning, Dia paused, his pen tapping against the paper.

"Got something?"

Dia started in his seat, his head snapping up. He had been so focused on his work that he had actually forgotten about Calix. How long had he been working? An hour? Two? And all that time the Fox had sat beside him, saying not a word. Had Dia truly gotten so absorbed that he had forgotten he was sitting beside a possible enemy?

"Well?" Calix's lips twitched in amusement as though he could tell exactly what the prince was thinking. It was a strange thought. Except with his mother and siblings Dia was used to keeping his expression guarded at all times but then 'usually' hardly extended to his bedroom in the middle of the night. Trying to ignore his unsettled feeling Dia turned his attention back to the paper in front of him, his pen tapping against it once more.

"I think it's book code."

The teasing expression slid from Calix's face as he too turned to eye the paper.

"Book code? Are you sure?"

Dia nodded. "As sure as I can be. I've tried every trick I know and I'm not getting anywhere, plus the format is perfect for giving page and word coordinates."

Calix drummed his fingers on the side of Dia's desk. "Can you crack it without the book?"

Dia shook his head. "Not by any method I know."

"Trickster..." The Fox swore softly as Dia sighed and leaned back in his chair, mentally echoing the sentiment.

"I don't suppose you happened to notice the titles of any of the queen's books while you were breaking into her rooms?"

Calix shook his head. "I was looking for correspondence, not reading materials."

Dia sighed again and rubbed at the side of his face. Now that he was no longer immersed in his work he was more aware of the spinning fog growing at the back of his mind. He should probably lie down again soon and drink more of his medicine to prevent a relapse.

"I'll try some common titles from the queen's home province tomorrow and if that doesn't work I'll go through everything she's gotten out of the royal library in the last year."

Calix arched an eyebrow at him. "Planning to ask her for a reading list?"

Dia raised his head and smiled sweetly up at the Fox. "I have my ways."

Calix's eyes widened slightly but then his lips curved in a sly grin. "I'm sure you do, after all you know an awful lot about code breaking for a prince without any political ambitions."

Dia shrugged. "Reclusive scholar remember? It's amazing what you can learn in the course of studying."

Calix chuckled softly. "Of course. How could I forget?"

He slid off of Dia's desk and stretched. "Well, Your Highness, scholars may keep unusual hours but guards have morning shifts."

"Really?" Dia tilted his head back to watch." You didn't seem to have a shift this morning. Was it your day off?"

Calix's lips quirked. "Tracking my movements?"

Dia smiled back. "Scholarly curiosity."

A surprised huff of laughter left the Fox's lips. "You know, the rumors don't do you justice Demiter."

"Which rumors are those?"

Calix arched an eyebrow at him. "You need to ask?"

Dia shook his head. No, he didn't. He knew exactly what rumors about him circulated through the court. He had planted most of them after all.

Calix turned in the direction of the window "I'll be back in a few days to see if you've cracked it."

"Alright. Come after dark. It's better that you don't draw attention to your visits."

"In that case I'll keep coming through your window. That way if anyone sees me it'll just reinforce our ruse from last night."

Dia started a little at that, suddenly hit by the sense memory of Calix's lips warm against his own. At the time he hadn't dwelt on it. It had been a means to an end. Calix had been a stranger and there had been far more important things consuming his mind, but now, with the Fox's word suddenly bringing the memory back to him Dia was surprised to feel a slight warmth in his cheeks. Quickly he cleared his throat. "That's probably best."

Calix turned back to him, a challenge in his golden eyes, "Unless a Demiter is too proud to let people think he's sleeping with a mere guard?"

Dia's eyes narrowed, irritation quickly replacing embarrassment. "Where would you get that idea?"

Calix shrugged lightly an unmistakable coldness entering his voice. "You're part of the ruling family. There's no telling what you'll decide is in your best interests, but you'll always put them first."

Dia stared coolly back. "You seem to have quite the dislike of the royal family for being a member of the guard."

Their gazes locked for a moment but then Calix shrugged again and turned back to the window. "A job as a job. A man has to eat."

Dia's eyes stayed locked on his back, studying the Fox as he reached for the window catch but as he pulled it open his short coat slid back a little, revealing part of the tattoo on his left wrist and Dia remembered his question from earlier in the day.

"Can I ask you something?"

Calix paused in the process of pushing the window open and turned back to look at Dia, his expression guarded.

"What?"

"I noticed your tattoo earlier. Is it a gender indicator? Or are you a follower of the Star Fox?"

Calix let out a soft breath and pushed up so that he was sitting perched on Dia's windowsill. "Gender of course. 'He' mostly but 'they' isn't incorrect either."

Dia considered him for a moment. "Why 'of course?'"

About to drop into the garden beyond Calix glanced back at him, a strangely bitter smile twisting the corners of his lips. "Demiter, I'm a soldier. What good is a god of peace to me?"

CHAPTER 6
BLOOD BELL

The junior librarian of the royal library had nearly lost his job two years before thanks to a bout of clumsiness which resulted in a bit of magically conjured flame having an unfortunate encounter with a lord's favorite book, a family heirloom he had lent to the library. The contents had not been damaged but the librarian had still broken the rule about no flames in the library. Normally he might have gotten away with a warning since it was his first offence, but the lord had been furious enough about the singed cover that he had demanded the librarian's immediate dismissal. Dia had intervened. The lord hadn't wanted his husband to learn about his relationship with a certain guard captain, and having someone with unfettered access to the royal archives and the treasury records in his debt had suited Dia well. The librarian was eager to show his gratitude to Dia on every possible occasion, so getting a list of everything the queen had checked out in the past year really was as simple as asking.

It was four days after his last meeting with Calix and

Dia was most of the way through the stack when Ruslan burst into his room.

"There you are!"

Dia turned in his seat, his whole body tensing when he caught sight of his brother's face.

"What's wrong?"

"It's Mirie. When I got back to the stables after training one of the grooms grabbed me. He said she was colicking and I should get you in case..." Ruslan's voice trailed away, fear bright in his dark gray eyes. Dia pushed himself away from his desk, his heart beginning to race. Mirie, his dapple gray mare, was one of the few gifts his royal father had ever given him. That alone might not have endeared her to Dia, but after years of partnership the idea of what 'just in case' could mean was enough to have him racing for the stables as fast as he could go.

When he reached it, Dia found the stables a hive of activity, grooms hurrying back and forth, arms laden with tack, the aisles filled with horses on crossties. The inside of the barn was a dim place. Fire was strictly forbidden there under any circumstances so it was lit only by the spring sun shafting in through doors and windows, and by a few individuals whose gifts allow them to conjure various forms of nonflammable light. The contrast between the sunny day outside and the dimness within meant that it took Dia a few moments to realize that not all the people filling the stables were grooms. Many of them were young people in their late teens or early twenties, a mixture of those in the fine clothes of the nobility and those in the black and gold of the guard, the unusual combination giving away what this must be. Even as he hurried inside Dia's eyes scanned the dimness until he caught sight of a small woman with long black hair dressed in an elegantly embroidered black and purple tunic and black riding britches. She was tightening the girth of an impatiently stomping chestnut mare, her hands moving deftly over the buckles. As though sensing his eyes on her the woman glanced in his direction then started, bright green eyes widening slightly at the sight of him.

"Prince Diamond." She inclined her head and Dia returned the gesture.

"Princess Emira." At Dia's side Ruslan bowed his head.

"I didn't know you were planning to join today's hunt." The princess's words were light and her expression gave nothing away, yet Dia could practically hear the thoughts racing behind the words. At nineteen, H'arn's crown princess was already a master of politics and intrigue, and she would already be trying to piece together what game her disinherited and reclusive half-brother might be playing by joining one of her hunts. Technically he was invited of course—Dia had a standing invitation, as he did to many other social functions of the palace city—but he had never accepted and so to do so now, without warning, could only be part of a plot.

"I'm not. A groom told my brother that my mare is ill."

"Ahh..." The princess's expression softened ever so slightly. "I'm sorry. What's wrong with her?"

"I'm not sure yet. I..."

"Princess!" The call came from behind Dia and he glanced over his shoulder to see Arya Omdare, caption of the princess's personal guard coming toward them. "Everyone's ready."

Princess Emira gave her a slight nod then her eyes flicked back to Dia. "I wish you and your horse luck, Prince."

"Enjoy your hunt, Princess." Dia inclined his head again

then hurried on, dodging around riders leading their horses to the entrance, Ruslan pressing close against his side. Not for the first time Dia felt a twinge in his stomach at the way Emira utterly ignored his younger siblings. He had never quite understood it. In any other member of the royal family he would've labeled it snobbishness yet, as the people now beginning to mount up in the outer yard were proof, Emira's social circle was wide and varied and even if they weren't royal Evren and Ruslan were still the children of an honored diplomat. Even if she didn't want to acknowledge them as her stepsiblings there was no reason for her to ignore them completely. Yet ignore them she always did.

"Prince!"

Dia waited for the last horse, an irritated bay mare who looked as though she probably kicked, to pass before hastening to the groom waving at him from beside Mirie's stall, all thoughts of the Crown Princess disappearing at the sight of his beloved mare. Her head was turned away from him biting at her own stomach as she pawed restlessly at her bedding with a front hoof, her ears twitching in distress and lather coating her neck.

"Good timing. The doctor should be here any moment."

"Will she be alright?" Ruslan asked, his eyes wide and worried.

The groom pursed her lips. "It's hard to say. If we knew what caused this treating it would be easier... Prince, have you noticed anything in the past few days?"

Dia shook his head. "I haven't been to the stables this week." The words felt heavy on his tongue. Between his health and his need to survive the queen's plot there hadn't been time but he should have come anyway. He should have found a way... Guilt clawing at his stomach Dia unlatched the stall and slipped inside. Mirie snorted and tossed her head but gave no other sign she had noticed him, continuing to paw at her disarrayed bedding. Dia laid a hand on her neck, gently stroking the sweat streaked coat, trying to calm her. They stayed like that for a few minutes until the doctor arrived then Dia stepped away to allow the woman space to examine the mare. As he did a flicker of red caught his eye and he knelt quickly to pull whatever it was from the shavings lining Mirie's stall. Dia straightened up then froze, staring at what he held.

"What do you have there?" It was the doctor who asked the question. "Is that blood bell?"

Dia nodded jerkily. It might be tattered and half trampled but the flower's scarlet bell-shaped pedals were unmistakable.

"How in the trickster's name did that get in here?" The doctor demanded, rounding on the groom. Dia barely heard them, a sudden roaring noise filling his ears.

Blood bell was a common flower, a weed, easily found throughout Tar Mel in the spring. It was also poisonous to horses and, precisely because it was so common, anyone who worked with horses in any capacity spent the entire spring working to keep their charges away from the plant by any means necessary. There was no way that a groom hired by the king to care for his own horses would be careless enough to bring so much as a petal of blood bell into the stables, so how had it gotten there?

"Dia, are you alright?" It was Ruslan who asked the question. Dia nodded jerkily, realizing that he'd just been standing frozen in Mirie's stall. Quickly he stepped back into the aisle, getting out of the way as the doctor began measuring out the antidote for blood bell poisoning. It was such a high risk in spring that she would always keep some in her travel bag and, assuming Mirie hadn't ingested an excessive amount of the flowers, she would be fine. No, her health was no longer Dia's worry. A horrible twisting in his stomach told the prince that he now had far bigger problems.

If blood bell didn't come to be in Mirie's stall accidentally then it was intentional, intentional at the same time his brother would be passing back through the stables at the end of his own daily riding lesson, intentional at the same time Princess Emira was readying her hunt.

Princess Emira...

Dia's head snapped toward the stable yard but to his horror he found it deserted, Emira and her companions had already gone and that meant...

"I need a horse!"

"What?" Ruslan looked up at him with wide eyes.

"Your Highness?" The groom also raised her head.

"A horse." Dia repeated. His breath was coming too fast, his heart hammering, his mind racing. "It doesn't matter whose horse, just tack up anyone fast and easy to handle."

"Your Highness." The groom looked uneasy now. "I can't just give you someone else's horse..."

"You can and you will! Now!" Panic gave Dia's voice a sharpness usually foreign to him and to his surprise he could hear the echo of his father in his voice. Maybe it was that which decided the groom because she inclined her head quickly.

"Yes Your Highness. Any horse?"

Dia nodded. "Any horse." Then, as she hurried away to the tack room, an idea struck him and he called after her, "No wait! Make sure the horse is big enough to carry two."

"Dia, what's going on?"

The prince spun back around to face his wide-eyed

brother. "You remember that friend I brought home? Calix? He's on shift at the Crown gate; I need you to get him for me!"

Ruslan started. "But if he's on shift..."

"It doesn't matter. Just bring him!"

Ruslan stared at him for a moment, then he nodded once and raced away.

Dia turned back in the direction of the groom. Every fiber of his being wanted to race after Emira the instant the horse was ready, but what good would it do to arrive in time if he was unable to act?

By the time Calix came running into view, a panting Ruslan trailing behind him, Dia was mounted on a large black gelding who pranced impatiently beneath him, clearly sensing his rider's distress.

"Get on!" Dia snapped, pulling the gelding up beside the mounting block as soon as the guard was within earshot. The Fox gave him an appraising look but, mercifully, didn't question him, just swung himself up behind Dia and wrapped his arms tightly around the prince's waist. The instant Dia felt him settle he turned the horse in the direction of the gate into the People's City and squeezed him into a rapid trot. It was impossible to post normally with another person pressed against his back, but fortunately the gelding's gait was smooth enough to sit to. Dia itched to push the horse into a canter, but even on the broad thoroughfare leading to the gate, while they were still in the city, he couldn't take the risk.

"Your Highness, this is hardly subtle."

The feeling of the Fox's breath against the back of his

ear made Dia start slightly but he ignored the strange sensation, focusing instead on the implied question.

"We're out of time for subtle."

"What happened?"

"Someone poisoned my horse to lure me to the stables at the same time Princess Emira was there getting ready for one of her hunts."

Calix swore. "You think the queen had her horse drugged?"

Dia nodded. "And made sure people would remember me being there, yes. I assume they'll say I poisoned my own horse as cover."

"Then why am I here? You could have warned her much faster without me."

Dia didn't answer immediately. They were approaching the gate between the Palace City and the People's City now and Dia raised his voice instead. "Clear the way!"

The heads of the guards and the people passing through the gate snapped up at the shout, and he saw startled eyes fix on him, but even at a distance the long silver-gray braid of Dia's hair, woven through with its customary purple ribbon, was distinctive enough that they hastily cleared out of the way without question. On the far side of the gate the main thoroughfare of Cylbra's Way was far more crowded with people but Dia wove the gelding through them as quickly as he could, relieved to find that the groom had been right to vouch for his temperament.

"I need you because Princess Emira is a cavalry-trained rider and it would be very sloppy of the queen to assume a riding accident would kill her."

"You think there's an assassin."

Dia could hear the dawning horror and understanding in the Fox's voice, and his stomach twisted as he nodded.

"If the princess's horse collapses it will stop the hunt. All of those riders gathering around, trying to figure out what happened?"

"Ambush." Calix let out a soft breath. "And you want me to kill the assassin for you."

It wasn't a question but Dia nodded anyway. "If I know the queen, she'll have given them some sort of forged papers to carry to make it look like I'm the one who hired them. If Emira's guards bring them down they're going to find whatever the queen has planted."

If we don't stop the assassin before they reach Emira I'm dead and all of these last six years will have been for nothing.

THE RIDE to the outer gates of Tar Mel seemed to take forever. Cylbra's Way might be the fastest way through the People's City but it was crowded with traffic. Carts filled with goods moved up and down the avenue, intermingled with the carriages of merchants and nobles. Messengers on horse or on foot darted back and forth across the way, weaving around the food vendors who set up their carts on the avenues edges and filled the air with their voices as they hocked their wares to all who passed. Usually when Dia descended into the People's City he couldn't help but lose himself among the crowds, buying snacks from the food vendors and taking a moment to observe the brightly colored chaos before venturing deeper into the city to find the book stalls or the mechanized workshops or the apothecary gardens. Today however, every second spent on Cylbra's Way only sent another spike of fear through him.

How long until the poison took effect in Emira's horse?

How long until the assassin made their move?

Were they already too late?

"Do you know where to go when we get out of here?" Calix asked the question against Dia's ear.

He nodded. "The princess's hunt always takes the same trail."

"Always? I'm surprised they catch anything then. The local wildlife must know to stay away by now."

"The princess's hunts aren't about hunting. She just likes to ride fast. Knowing the trail means she knows where it's safe to gallop." Around the court, Princess Emira's 'hunts' were often spoken of as a sort of challenge only skilled riders dared attempt. It was that level of notoriety which meant Dia knew exactly where they needed to go. Yet it was also, no doubt, that level of notoriety which had allowed the queen to set her trap.

Heart racing in a way that, for once, had nothing to do with his illness, Dia guided the gelding around a slower moving cart crammed with crates, and then, at last, they were at the gate. He dug in his heels and the horse, already on edge with his riders distress, darted forward, breaking to a canter as soon as they passed beneath the arch. Dia leaned forward, pressing himself low over the gelding's withers to minimize wind resistance and felt the Fox tighten his grip as he leaned into Dia's back. The prince had ridden with his stepfather when he was a child and some-times with his siblings when they were young, but he had never shared a saddle with another adult and the sensation was strange and unwieldy. Calix's arms were tight around Dia's stomach and his balance felt wrong. For a moment he worried that, without the stirrups to balance his feet against, Calix would fall and take Dia down with him, but the Fox's legs must have been strong because they kept him in the saddle and he made no sound of distress. Dia decided to trust him to manage his own weight and concentrated on pushing the horse to extend his stride.

Dia might never have joined any of the princess's hunts, the risk of his illness flaring while surrounded by so many strangers far too great, but he had ridden in this direction many times, first with his stepfather and then with his mother and younger siblings. He knew the trails well. From the gate they took the first right hand fork in the road, veering south into the forested hills which encircled most of Tar Mel. From there they would ride on for nearly a mile until they would reach a three-pronged fork in the road. As they approached the fork Dia expected every turn and twist of the road to reveal something, a messenger riding back for help, the fallen body of a horse or maybe even the hunting party gathered around their dead princess. But with every turn the road revealed nothing. Then the fork was before them and Dia didn't hesitate to turn the gelding on to the narrower right-hand trail.

"Are you sure this is the way?" Calix hissed the question into Dia's ear. The prince could hardly blame him. While the forest road they had been on before continued wide and well-trodden, this new way was narrow and slightly over-grown, and Dia could feel the gelding gathering himself as he struggled to maintain his pace up the slope.

"A shortcut." Dia dug his heels into the horse's side but he could feel the gelding slowing all the same. "The horse is too tired carrying both of us. We'll never catch up on the main trail."

The gelding crested the rise and Dia kicked him forward, pushing him into one last burst of energy. Below them now and more winding he could see the main track curving around the base of the slope and then at last...

"There!"

Dia pointed downward to a cluster of horses and riders halted on the main trail but before he had a chance to do anything more than glimpse them Calix shouted as well.

"Demiter, look!"

For a moment Dia couldn't figure out what Calix was talking about but then he saw and his heart seemed to stop. A little way down the slope, hidden from below by an outcropping of boulders, stood an archer, his bow already bent. Then everything happened at once. Dia's moment of inattention was enough to allow the exhausted gelding to stumble to a walk and the shock of the transition together with Calix's unaccustomed weight sent the prince rocking forward onto the horse's neck. The momentum sent Calix listing dangerously sideways, but rather than do anything to steady himself Dia felt the Fox's arms release from around him. The next instant there was a crash as Calix hit the ground rolling, the motion taking him over the side of the slope down toward the assassin who started at the sudden noise even as he released his arrow. There was a cry from below and then Dia was throwing himself from the saddle, his feet slipping on the spring growth even as there was another shout from below. This time it sounded like anger rather than pain, but the prince didn't have time to focus on it because the assassin was spinning back toward him, already notching another arrow. For an instant Dia froze staring down the shaft, feeling the breath catch in his lungs. Then there was a flash of orange and Calix was leaping up from the ground, somehow turning his roll into a lunge as he threw himself at the assassin.

The arrow snapped from the bowstring, going high and wide as the assassin stumbled back. Yet he must have been well-trained indeed because he recovered in an instant, swinging the bow down and around like a club and Calix, in his hurry to keep the assassin from shooting Dia, hadn't had a chance to draw his own weapons. The blow collided with the side of the Fox's shoulder and he stumbled back with a gasp, giving the assassin space to drop the bow and draw his short sword. The blade flashed up and out in a draw cut that Calix was too close to avoid. Dia heard the sound of ripping fabric and a soft cry from the Fox's lips, and then he was running, boots slipping on the spring growth as he jerked his dagger from its sheath.

At the sound of approaching footsteps, the assassin glanced in Dia's direction. It was only for a fraction of a second but it was enough. Calix twisted away from his distracted opponent and, in the same movement drew the two blades hanging at his waist, sword in his right hand dagger in his left. Dia was surprised to realize that the Fox's sword was actually a rapier, slimmer and more delicate than the hand-and-a-half swords typically carried by the guard but an instant later, as Calix lunged at the assassin, Dia understood why. The Fox was fast, twisting to catch the assassin's next strike against his rapier so that the assassin's blade slid down his own, using the momentum to push him off balance even as Calix brought the dagger up toward his ribs. The assassin jumped backwards just in time but Calix was already there, starting in with a flurry of blows which the assassin only just managed to deflect. He brought his knee up in a savage blow which should have landed right between Calix's legs but the Fox darted back just in time. The assassin lunged forward, pressing his advantage. Calix's left wrist snapped and for a moment Dia thought that the Fox had thrown his dagger but, no, it was still in his hand. What shot up from his palm were the stars. The glowing spheres of light were considered one of the most minor of gifts, good for illuminating darkness and nothing more, but now, thrust into the assassin's face they became a weapon, sudden and blinding. The assassin lurched back, eyes squinting in the sudden light, and that was all the opening Calix needed. Dia had thought on the day they met that the Fox was a killer and it seemed he had been right because Calix didn't hesitate for a moment to drive both sword and dagger deep into the assassin's body.

The man gave a gurgling cry and slumped forward, struggling to pry himself from Calix's blades even as his own sword slipped from his fingers. With a hiss of effort Calix pulled the blades free and the man dropped to his knees, swayed for a moment, reaching out beseechingly toward Calix, then collapsed face forward onto the ground, blood seeping into the dirt around him. Dia felt the bile rise sharp and sudden in his throat. He had seen the dead before but he had never seen death, not like this, not bloody and gasping and struggling for life and for a moment all Dia could do was stand there wrestling with the sudden churning of his stomach. Slowly, Calix turned back toward him, blades still raised and soaked in blood. There was blood splattered across his short coat as well and even a few flecks of crimson splashed across one cheek. In that instant he looked wild and terrible—Adjra, goddess queen of battles, come to walk the earth. Their eyes met, pale gray finding gold which was for once utterly devoid of light, a gold empty of everything but death.

"There! Behind the outcropping!"

It was a cry from below which broke the moment, snapping Dia back into the wider reality, a reality in which the assassin had gotten off at least one arrow in the direction of Emira's hunt, a reality in which his death had been far from silent. Suddenly Dia was moving again, forcing all thoughts of his twisting stomach aside as he threw himself at the assassin's body. There was so much blood and he couldn't even be sure if the man was fully dead but there wasn't time for that, not now. Shoving his dagger back into its sheath, Dia tore frantically into the assassins short coat, ignoring the blood which stained his fingers as he searched the fabric until something crinkled slightly beneath his touch. Stuffing his hand under the man's jacket he forced his fingers into an inner pocket and pulled out a set of crumpled papers. He could hear footsteps now, approaching far too fast so he didn't have time to look, just shoved them into the waist of his own trousers and glanced up, searching for a place to hide. His eyes caught on Calix still standing, blades drawn, just beside the body. Kneeling with his eyes level with the Fox's stomach Dia saw now, what, with all the assassin's blood, he had missed before. He had been right when he thought he heard fabric rip earlier. There was a tear in Calix's short coat just above the right hip, and beneath the ruined black fabric, tattered white cloth had been dyed crimson.

"You're hurt!" Dia scrambled back to his feet, taking an instinctive step toward Calix who gave a dismissive shake of his head then swayed slightly. Dia grabbed his forearm to steady him. "Here, let me…"

Calix stiffened, eyes going to a point over Dia's shoulder and the prince instinctively whipped around to find himself staring down the drawn blade of Arya Omdare, captain of the princess's guard.

They were caught.

CHAPTER 7
THE MESSAGE

"Prince Diamond." The captain's voice was sharp with surprise but the blade in her hand didn't waiver for an instant even as she took them in: Calix, blades drawn and soaked in crimson, Dia with his hands covered in blood, and the assassin lying dead at their feet beside his bow. Quickly Calix shook off Dia's hand and shouldered his way in front of the prince, his blades providing a wall of steel between Dia and the captain. Dia could feel his heart racing, feel his breath coming far too quickly, feel the assassin's papers pressing against the waistband of his trousers and the horrible, too-warm sensation of blood on his fingers, but none of that could matter now. He had to get this situation under his control, because if he didn't, if Captain Omdare came to the conclusion that Dia was behind this attempt on her princess's life, then all of this would have been for nothing.

The Princess.

The arrow the assassin had managed to loose.

Could he have...

Dia studied the captain's face.

No. She was angry, yes, her gaze hard and suspicious, but it lacked the uncontrollable fury he would've expected to see there if Emira was dead. That meant they still had a chance.

"Captain Omdare?" Dia forced his eyes to widen in surprise in his voice to rise in startled confusion. "What are you doing here?"

The captain frowned slightly but her gaze was as hard as ever. "I could ask you the same question."

"Watch your tone when you speak to His Highness!" Calix's interjection was sudden and sharp enough to make Dia start, his eyes flicking to the Fox who still stood half in front of him, weapons drawn, sounding nothing like the cunning blackmailer who had teased and bated and mocked Dia since the moment they met. Now his voice was hard with a righteous fury that made him sound as though he was Dia's own bodyguard.

Clever Fox.

"Calix, it's alright." Dia rested a hand on his shoulder as though to soothe him. "You can stand down."

The Fox nodded and slowly lowered his weapons, the very picture of loyal obedience.

"Now, Captain Omdare..."

There was a rustling in the leaves and two more members of the princess's guard appeared through the trees. Behind them, hand resting on the hilt of her belt knife and dirt staining her black and purple riding costume, came the princess herself. All three stopped abruptly at the sight before them but Dia only caught the slightest flicker of surprise in Emira's face before it was gone again, masked by cool consideration.

"Prince Diamond, this is an unexpected surprise." Emira stepped between her guards to stand at Captain

Omdare's side. The dirt suggested that whatever the queen had drugged her horse with had resulted in a fall but if the princess was injured her movements didn't show it.

"Your Highness." Dia inclined his head. "I did not realize your hunt was so nearby."

"Oh?" The princess's gaze flicked from Dia to the dead man at his feet and back up again. "What a coincidence. I also did not realize you were nearby. Your horse must have recovered *quite* swiftly."

Emira's green eyes were cold and filled with suspicion, and Dia knew that there was no excuse he could give that she would believe. For a moment he hesitated, wondering if there might be a chance here, a chance to tell her the truth, use the assassin's body and the papers as evidence, and convince her that the queen was a danger to them both. Yes, it would all come down to the queen. If Emira viewed her as a rival or political adversary then his words and evidence would be enough, but if she didn't, if she viewed her stepmother as the mother of her heart? If that was the case then anything he said would only seem like a desperate attempt to cast blame away from himself. Dia alone among the royal family did not live within the Crown. He was utterly cut off from the inside drama and details of their lives. He had no sense of their relationships, and Emira, reserved as she had always been, had never given any public sign one way or the other. Maybe if Dia had been desperate he would have taken the gamble, but there was still the letter Calix had copied, still a chance for concrete proof, proof he wouldn't be able to find if he was behind bars.

"She's recovering." Dia gave the princess a small sheepish smile. "But I was still rather upset so Calix and I decided to borrow a mount and go for a ride to get my mind off of things. I knew your hunt would be taking the main trail so we decided to take this one. For privacy..." Dia shot a quick glance in Calix's direction, hoping that it and the discomfort in his tone would cover for the fact that he wasn't able to blush on command. After being caught kissing in the aviary there had to be rumors about the reclusive prince having a lover among the guard. Emira was a master of court intrigue so she had to have heard. The implication should be enough.

"I see.." Emira's gaze barely flickered in Calix's direction. "But it seems your outing was disrupted."

"We were." Dia forced his eyes to widen and his voice to tremble slightly. His mind flicked to the sight of the assassin falling to the ground, the sound of his dying breaths, the feel of his blood, warm and wet beneath Dia's fingers, and found that the feigned distress came all too easily. "I don't know who he was. Maybe some sort of bandit? We found him bending his bow and when he saw us he attacked."

"A bandit? So close to Tar Mel?"

Dia shrugged helplessly. "I don't know. He never said anything." Inwardly he winced, knowing how foolish he sounded, but it was the best he could do in the moment. Let the princess think him upset and easily rattled. Let her think him weak. Let her think him anything she wanted, as long as it bought them time.

"I see..." Emira's green gaze remained hard and full of suspicion. Dia couldn't tell whether she was buying his distress or not. Either way she was unlikely to accept anything he said as truth. Yet with whatever documentation the queen had provided the assassin safely hidden beneath Dia's vest she couldn't be sure Dia was plotting against her either, not when he and Calix had so obviously slain her hunt's attacker. She would want to investigate thoroughly and that would take time, days hopefully. Hopefully long enough for Dia to crack the code and get the evidence he needed. "In that case it seems I have the pair of you to thank for saving us from him."

"It was our pleasure."

"My guards will take care of the body. Do you or your ... companion require water or medical supplies? I can have one of my guards bring some up if you don't want to join us?"

Dia's eyes flicked to Calix who gave a slight shake of his head.

"Thank you for the offer, Princess, but we are fine. I think I would prefer to just return to Tar Mel." Again he let his voice shake slightly, hoping that his words would be read as another sign of his distress rather than a desire to remove them from her observation as quickly as possible.

The princess eyed Dia for another moment then nodded slightly. "Very well. Whatever you wish."

Dia inclined his head. "Then we will be going."

THE RIDE back to the city took much longer than their earlier journey. Dia had found the gelding grazing by the side of the trail. Mercifully he hadn't stepped on his reins despite Dia's failure to tie them up, so while too tired for any speed he was in good enough shape to let them both ride him back as long as they kept to a walk. Before catching the horse, Calix had offered his already ruined short coat and Dia had used the fabric to wipe as much of the drying blood from his hands as he could. Then Dia had tied the coat around the Fox in an attempt to stop the bleeding. They didn't speak much on the ride back, just enough to agree that the last thing they needed was the sort of official investigation which would follow if Calix turned up at the clinic with a sword wound. Otherwise Dia spent the journey lost in thought, trying to decide what Emira's next move would be and how long it would take for the queen to organize another attempt. Two days? Three? The clock was getting perilously close to midnight, but it wasn't there yet. He still had a chance.

DIA DIDN'T RETURN the gelding to the stables himself. Riding past the gate guards had been one thing—they had only needed a glance to recognize the prince and after that their eyes had moved on to more suspicious travelers. But the amount of blood still covering both of them would not be missed by anyone who looked closely after they dismounted, and after the demands he had shouted in the stables earlier, Dia was sure that the grooms would be curious enough to look closely. Instead they rode directly to Dia's home where he asked Ruslan to return the horse for him. His brother's eyes had burned with curiosity as he surveyed them both but mercifully he had kept his questions to himself while Dia asked Evren for the medical kit. They hadn't asked questions either, just looked at him with worry and grief in their eyes before they had gotten it and Dia had winced at the sight, seeing the ghost of their father's death in that look. He wanted to reassure them, wanted to promise them that things would end differently this time, but that was a promise he couldn't make and so he only thanked them and ushered Calix away.

Alone together in Dia's room, the prince placed the stiff

leather bag with its medical supplies on his desk and opened it, searching through it for bandages, ointment, and a small bottle of alcohol. Then he turned back to Calix and froze. While Dia had been busy with the medical kit, the Fox had untied his short coat and removed his shirt leaving him bare from the waist up. The Fox's body was all pale skin and wiry muscle but that wasn't what drew the soft gasp from Dia's lips. No, it was the scars. Calix's lower torso, his sides, shoulders and arms, all were covered in a crisscrossing map of scars. Darker splashes of skin suggested burns while thin lines suggested knives, and a few thicker markings, the touch of swords. There was even a puckered mark just below his right shoulder which suggested an arrow wound and along his left side a reddish wheal that might've been left by the stroke of a whip.

On his upper chest there were two more scars, but those Dia recognized as the curving marks of chosen surgery so he paid them no attention, eyes fastening instead on the other marks, marks that were definitely not voluntary. Yet even in that mess of scars Calix's new injuries stood out. The bruise on the Fox's shoulder from where the assassin had struck him with his bow was already darkening to purple, a few lighter bruises on his right side showed where he had fallen from the horse, and on his left side the blood had dried dark and flaking around his wound. Dia just kept staring. He couldn't help it. He had never seen so many scars on one person before, and Calix wasn't some grizzled graybeard with decades of battle experience behind him. He was only nineteen, two years younger than Dia. What kind of life had he lived to end up like this? What had he been through? How much had he suffered?

Eyes still fixed on that map of scars, Dia unconsciously took a step forward, then another, reaching out until his fingertips brushed the scarred skin of Calix's side. The Fox tensed, and the feel of the slight motion beneath his fingers was enough to jolt Dia back into reality. Hastily he jerked his hand back, eyes widening as they snapped up to Calix's face.

"I'm sorry. I shouldn't have done that!"

Calix looked away. "It's fine."

Dia shook his head, embarrassed color rising to his cheeks. "No, it isn't. I shouldn't have touched you without asking."

"I said it's fine." Calix still wasn't looking at him but there was a slight edge to his voice now.

Dia's heart twisted. Until that point it had been easy to think of Calix only as "the Fox," a cunning, mocking black-mailer, an ally of convenience who's cleverness he might enjoy but whose death or banishment he might one day have to arrange. But now... It was impossible to look at all those scars crisscrossing Calix's body and not see a man who had already lived through far too much—someone who had suffered in countless ways, someone who had been hurt over and over again and yet kept getting back up, someone who had been wounded again today for Dia's sake. As the Prince silently poured water from a flask onto a bit of cloth and began gently dabbing at the dried blood around the wound he recalled the moment: the assassin with his bow drawn and his arrow aimed directly at Dia's throat, Calix lunging upward from the ground, knocking the arrow away. The Fox was a canny fighter, fast, ruthless and clearly experienced. Once he'd drawn his weapons the assassin hadn't been able to touch him. The only reason he had been wounded was because he threw himself on the assassin with his blades still sheathed. The only reason he had been wounded was because he had taken a risk to save Dia's life.

The prince put down the now-stained cloth and picked up the bottle of alcohol.

"This is going to hurt." Dia said it gently.

Calix nodded and gestured for him to continue.

Carefully Dia poured a bit of the alcohol over Calix's side. The Fox hissed in pain, his hands curling into fists, but he said nothing, allowing Dia to finish his work, applying pinkish cream to the wound and wrapping the Fox's lower torso in bandages. All throughout the process Calix remained uncharacteristically silent leaving Dia's mind free to wander from the scars on his body to the fight in the forest and back again. Calix had taken the wound before he had ever drawn his blades. It wasn't a life-threatening wound certainly, but it was more than just a scratch. Calix had been fighting injured that entire time, yet he had still been fast and fluid and deadly, so much so that Dia had to wonder: how many times had he fought while already injured? How many times had he had to force his own pain aside and raise his sword to protect his life? What had he been through to turn him into this, this killer covered in the marks of his own suffering? Who had done this? Who had hurt him like this?

"If I asked what happened to you, would you tell me?"

Calix started a little at the question as though he had been lost in his own thoughts, but then he shook his head. "No."

Dia had expected the answer so he only nodded in acceptance. Perhaps he shouldn't have, perhaps he should have continued to poke and prod until the Fox gave something away. After all, Calix knew so many of Dia's secrets and Dia knew so very little about him. There might even have been some justice in it, fair play for Calix pushing him to reveal the truth of his illness. Yet with his newfound awareness of Calix still washing over him, the only question Dia found himself wanting to ask was, "Why did you protect me?"

Calix shrugged lightly. "I'm a royal guard. It's my job."

"Oh really? Because you don't seem to think much of the royal family."

Calix shifted slightly. "Like I said before, it's a job."

Dia eyed him consideringly, a sudden thought coming to him. "But why is it your job?"

"What do you mean?" Calix was good at masking his responses, but with Dia's fingers still busy bandaging his side the prince couldn't fail to notice the way the Fox tensed slightly at the question.

"I saw your skills today. You could be a mercenary or a soldier, or if you wanted to be a guard you could go anywhere. Yet you chose to be here, guarding a family you hate."

Calix let out a soft breath. "It's complicated."

Dia glanced up from his work, hands stilling on the bandages as he took in the exhaustion in the Fox's eyes. It was a look unlike any Dia had seen on Calix's face before, lacking mischief or mockery, or even the deadly intent that the prince had seen there after the Fox had killed the assassin and Dia ached at the sight of it.

Gently he asked, "How is it complicated?"

"There's something I need to do in Tar Mel so I need a job that lets me stay here. It doesn't matter how I feel about the job."

Dia started at that. He had been expecting another evasion or an outright refusal to elaborate, yet instead Calix had answered him. Why? Maybe it had something to do with the exhaustion in the Fox's eyes? Was he weary of carrying whatever this was? Or was it simply that playing the role of the loyal guard to a family he so clearly disliked was taking a toll on him?

"Why do you need to stay in Tar Mel?"

The corners of Calix's lips curved in a small, bitter, smile. "I have a responsibility I need to fulfill."

"A responsibility?"

Calix nodded but said nothing more, and Dia could sense that even if he pressed he would get no more details, so instead he asked a different question.

"Did you protect me because you thought if I was shot it might somehow result in you having to leave Tar Mel?"

Dia expected Calix to agree so he was surprised when the Fox shook his head.

"Then why?"

Calix looked away, and when he spoke again his voice was quiet.

" I just didn't want to watch you die."

"Oh..." The word left Dia's lips on a quiet breath, his eyes widening as something unfamiliar shifted in his chest. For a moment he just looked at Calix. Then he turned his eyes back to the bandages, continuing to wrap them around the Fox's lower abdomen. As he pulled yet another loop of bandaging into place Dia spoke quietly. "Thank you."

The Fox nodded in acknowledgment but said nothing, his eyes fixing vaguely in the direction of Dia's window.

In silence the prince finished layering the bandage, then fastened it in place with a bit of metal before stepping back to survey his work.

"How does that feel?"

The Fox said nothing, eyes still unfocused as though lost in thought.

Dia frowned, a prickle of unease running through him. "Calix?"

"Why do you want to be king?"

Dia froze, his breath catching as the concern he had felt moments before disappeared beneath the shock of sudden panic. Outside the great clock at the top of the Crown chimed the hour.

"What?"

"Why do you want to be king?" Calix repeated the question, at last turning back to Dia, an odd light glowing in his golden eyes. "You let everyone think you're a scholar recluse with no interest in power or court games, but we both know that's a lie. Your health is a dangerous secret that could destroy you if it ever got out which is why you hide yourself. I assume it's also why you've never gone with your mother on any of her diplomatic missions back to Sinotalya. You can't risk the rest of the travel party noticing that there's something wrong, but that only matters if you're planning to come back and continue gaining power in court. It's clear the family you love isn't your royal one, and your mother is the niece of the governor of Sinotalya. The queen only wants you dead because she thinks you're a possible threat, but Sinotalya is on the other side of the mountains, and if you took your siblings and went to join your mother's family, you'd be removing yourself enough not to be a threat anymore. You could live out your life peacefully there without the political games which make you live in fear of anyone finding out your sick. And, you're smart enough to know all of that, so why stay?"

"You asked me why I'm here, but why are *you* here? You don't have an official role in court to stay for, you don't have lovers or friends, your life is in danger because the queen thinks you're a threat, and I saw the way the princess looked at you today. She also suspects you could be one. There's no reason for you to stay and let them think of you as a possible rival for the throne unless you *are* a rival for the throne. But why?" Calix gestured around them from Dia's clothes, well-made but simple, to the furnishings of his room, much the same. "If you just wanted it for the wealth or the status you wouldn't be living like this. So I'll ask again: why do you want to be king?"

For a moment all Dia could do was stare, his heart pounding, his mind racing as he thought through and discarded possible lies. Calix was an unknown force, someone who had only been in his life for a matter of days, a blackmailer who had caught him in one secret which could destroy him and forced him into revealing the second. He should not give him the third.

And yet...

And yet behind his eyes Dia saw again Calix throwing himself on the assassin, saving Dia's life, one more scar for the map covering the man's body. He had risked himself for Dia. He had come when Dia asked and he had killed for him.

'I just didn't want to watch you die.'

The words rang again through Dia's memory, an acknowledgment that given only a moment to think and choose, Calix had acted to protect Dia even though he must have known the injury it would cost him. The thought stirred an echo deep in Dia, a memory utterly different and yet... And yet. The memory clung to Dia as it always did, the guilt a constant weight that had followed him through all of the last five years. Now, again, someone had tried to aid him, and now, again, that person had been hurt for it.

Dia didn't know what Calix was fighting for, what " responsibility" compelled him to remain in Tar Mel at any cost. An employer? A family member? A friend? A lover? Yet staring at the scars covering Calix's body, some part of Dia ached to trust him, to confide in him this final secret which not even his siblings knew. Dia had been doing this alone for so long, carrying this alone for so long. Yet today he hadn't been alone. Today when he had needed help he had called for Calix, and Calix had come. Dia had asked Calix to kill for him and Calix had done it. Wasn't that worth something? And if Calix was going to continue associating with him, didn't he deserve to understand the full magnitude of the risk?

"Alright." Dia took a shuddering breath. "I'll show you."

Dia crossed to his nightstand and picked up his coded journal and brought it back over to the desk. Finding the page was easy. It was thicker than the rest and he knew at the moment his fingers brushed against it.

"This is why."

He stepped aside to allow Calix to see the page. The Fox took two steps closer to the desk then froze, his entire body stiffening, shock for once written clearly across his features.

"That's..." Even his voice had changed, hoarse and strangled by the sight before him.

"Blood." Dia finished quietly. He could hardly blame Calix for his reaction. Even for a soldier it was one thing to kill in the heat of battle and another to be surprised by a sight like this. A small piece of metal had been inserted into the page of Dia's notebook, bolting a piece of fabric to the paper. The fabric itself was tattered and smoke stained. Scrawled across it, in what was clearly the sender's own blood, were two desperate words. "Help us."

"When I was thirteen my father struck an alliance with the two queens of Avarniy." Dia began quietly, his eyes still fixed on the bloodstained fabric. "They were afraid that

Estron would invade and that they didn't have the power to force them back. My father was always looking for any advantage in our war against Estron. He liked the idea of having access to goods from Avarniy's ports and he didn't like the idea of their rich farmland falling into the hands of Estron, so he pledged our military to their protection. When the negotiations began, the queens came in person to Tar Mel to meet with my father. They brought their three daughters with them, Avery, Dawn, and Lyra. My father assigned me to be their companion and guide during their visit, and we became friends. During the next two years, while the alliance held, they visited a few times. I even gave them one of my messenger falcons so we could keep in contact. They didn't know about my secret, my health, but outside of my family they were still the first real friends I'd ever had. We were close. And then the invasion..."

The invasion. For decades Palia, the nation on H'arn's eastern border had kept itself out of the wars which engulfed so much of the continent so no one had expected its change of policy and the way its army had swept south, burning their way through Avarniy too fast for its ally H'arn to come to its aid. At least that was the official story.

"Everyone thinks that we were caught off guard by the invasion, but it isn't true. I don't know which one of the siblings sent me that message, but when I got it I ran straight to my father and told him that something must be terribly wrong. He said he already knew. I demanded that he send help and that's when he told me about the attack, told me that he knew the attack was coming because he cut a deal with Palia. They wanted Avarniy's farmland for themselves so they told my father that if he had our army stand aside and let them conquer Avarniy they would break the rest of their neutrality and ally with us against Estron.

Unlike Avarniy, Palia had a real army and could make a difference for us in the war, so my father agreed and Avarniy burned. I know everyone blames Palia for the Burning of Avarniy, but the truth is my father is just as responsible. He could have stopped it but he decided he cared more about conquering just a bit more of Estron than about the thousands of Avarniy civilians who he had sworn to protect. He didn't even regret it. He just told me to grow up and that sometimes sacrifices needed to be made for victory, as though the population of an entire nation didn't matter. He told me that it was my own fault for getting too attached to foreigners..."

Dia could feel his shoulders shaking, his eyes blurring, memories rising up like a wave as they always did when he stared at that fabric for too long. He took a breath, forcing himself to calm, letting hard determination replace his pain.

"That was the day I decided I wanted the throne. H'arn is one of the two most powerful nations on the continent, one of the most powerful nations in the world, and I can't let that man or any successor he picks be in control of it. If they are I know it will just happen again. I won't let it happen again, not when there's even a chance I can stop it. That's why I have to be king."

For a long time there was silence between them as they both stood looking at that bloodstained scrap of fabric, the room so quiet that Dia could hear the ticking of his pocket watch. At last, when he heard Calix take a step closer to him Dia finally turned to face his companion.

"Well? Will you turn me in as a traitor?"

Calix stared back at him, his face pale and a strange light burning in his golden eyes.

"Do you mean it?"

Dia nodded, his eyes meeting Calix's unflinchingly. "Every word."

"Then as long as you stay on this path, you will have my support *and* my silence."

Dia felt the weight of those words hit him with their implication, not just support but silence, silence not just on this, but on everything. For a moment all he could do was stare back into Calix's golden eyes. He had no reason to trust those words and yet, in that moment, he did.

Slowly he inclined his head.

"Thank you."

CHAPTER 8
THE SPY

"*According to centuries of research, the thing that differentiates the worlds is magic. Each world's magic seems to function according to its' own laws. Unlike our own, there are worlds where everyone is born with magic and other worlds where only some are born with the capacity for the gift, leaving the rest of those worlds' inhabitants utterly without even the chance at a gift. In fact, I have found in my research that the way our gifts pass through inheritance upon a loved one's death is not only not typical in other worlds, but may even be unique to our own. Certainly I have never seen reference to it in the notes of any explorer or diplomat whose writings I have had access to.*

Similarly, while we on Fourth draw all of our gifts from cosmic energy and are, therefore, limited in our magic to the forms that energy can take, this does not appear to be the case in other worlds. I have read accounts of worlds where those with the gift can manipulate ice, shift their bodies into those of birds, and even see the future. There are even accounts of our enemies during the Dragons' War manipulating the very sound we hear and the very air we breathe the same way some of our gifted can control flame and lightning. It makes me wonder if the collapse of economic prosperity which began the Crimson Age was not only caused by our loss of the war and the sealing of the world gates, but also by the loss of access to other worlds' magics which might have stabilized our agriculture and industry. Perhaps restoration of those gifts could be what we need to end this age of blood. But I also know there is little point to such speculation. The magics of other worlds lie beyond the gates, and the gates have been sealed for two hundred years. Knowing what harm we did when they were open, perhaps it is for the best."

-From the writings of Prince Diamond Havoran Demiter

"Dia, can I talk to you?" Dia turned his head to find Evren watching him with worried brown eyes. He was laying on the cushioned daybed which sat in the garden behind the house, sheltered beneath arching tree bows. It was early afternoon and he'd only been awake for a few hours. He'd spent most of the night attempting to decode the queen's message, Calix seated beside him helping him to keep track of which book and page combinations he'd already tried and reminding him to occasionally eat and drink. They had also examined the bloodstained pages Dia had taken from the assassin.

He had been right. The papers appeared to be orders for Princess Eimira's assassination written in a near perfect forgery of his hand, but other than confirming the prince's suspicions, they were of little help. Calix had asked if they could perhaps learn something incriminating by trying to trace how the queen had gotten her hands on enough samples of Dia's handwriting for her forger to copy from, but the prince had only shaken his head. The advent of the printing press might have done away with the need for handwritten books, but the original hand-penned copies of all of his scholarly papers were still stored in the library. Dia could and would speak to his helpful librarian about seeing the records of all of his work's recent check outs in order to attempt to trace the queen's forger, but if the forger had only looked through the papers without ever removing them from the library, then there would be no record of them. With that possibility in mind Dia and Calix had turned their attention back to the coded letter.

Despite the mounting urgency of his decryption, the danger from the queen and now, possibly, from the princess as well, Dia had found the whole evening oddly peaceful. He wasn't used to having someone to work alongside, especially not someone that he could talk to freely, and the experience had been... He wasn't sure he had a word for what it had been, but he couldn't help wanting to spend another evening like that, probably more than one—just without the looming danger. Unfortunately they had found nothing. Whatever book the queen and her sister had used for their cipher, it was not one of the ones she had checked out of the library in the last year. Dia and Calix had agreed they only had one option remaining, another secret trip into the queen's quarters to search her bookshelves. They had planned to meet at sundown by the gate of the Queens garden and proceed from there, leaving Dia to spend the afternoon resting with his bottle of medicine to ensure he would be well enough.

At Evern's question Dia shifted a little higher up on his pillows and gestured for them to take the empty seat next to the daybed. They did so, hands dropping into their lap and fingers curling and uncurling slightly in the way Evren always did when worried about something. The sight was enough to send worry sparking through Dia's own chest too.

"Ev, what's wrong?"

Evren took a quick breath and met his eyes steadily, their gaze troubled and filled with shadows.

"What's going on?"

Dia stiffened at the question. Part of him had been expecting it ever since he'd asked them for the doctors' kit the previous day, but that didn't mean he had a good answer ready, or at least not one he wanted to give, not to Evren.

Maybe that wasn't fair. Maybe he owed them an explanation. But still... If knowing somehow put them at risk then...

"Talk to me?" Evren's voice was gentle as it cut through his thoughts. There was a heaviness to it that he had heard there now and then over the last five years, a weight of age and knowledge that they were far too young to carry, a weight they only carried because of him.

He hesitated for another moment then shook his head. "I think it's better I don't. There are some things it's safer you don't know. You know that."

They bit their bottom lip, hands still opening and closing as though conflicted about something. "Dia..." They hesitated again then, seeming to come to a decision, they let out a soft breath and continued. "I know what really happened to father."

Dia bolted upright so fast that the world spun and he had to lean forward, steadying himself with his palms pressed flat against the daybed.

"How?"

Evren's eyes dropped to their hands and they buried their fingers in the folds of their skirt. "I've always known. I heard you and father and mother talking, the night before he left. I didn't understand all of it at the time but after... Afterward, when I looked at the map and saw where he had been assigned I realized how strange it was and…" Their voice trailed away and they shrugged. "I don't know everything but I know enough."

"I'm sorry." Dia whispered the words. He could feel the color draining from his face, feel a dizziness wash over him that for once had nothing to do with his illness. He should say more, he knew that, so much more. He owed it to Evren, and to Ruslan too, but what else could he say? What words could ever be enough to make up for the loss of a father?

Evren shook their head, a quick, birdlike motion. "It wasn't your fault."

"It was." The guilt rose up in Dia again, a rapidly swelling tide which threatened to pull him under. "I should never have gotten him involved."

"That's why you never tell me anything, isn't it?" Evren raised their head to study him, sadness flickering in their dark eyes. "You're afraid of getting me involved."

Unable to find words for the depth of his fears, Dia simply nodded.

"I'm not a child anymore, you know? I'm fourteen."

Fourteen. One year younger than Dia was when he received the bloody message which had rewritten the course of his life. One year older than Dawn had been when she died. Three years older than Lyra had been when she died.

"Mother wouldn't want me to put you at risk."

Evren's gaze hardened slightly. "Did she tell you that?"

Dia shook his head. Their mother was currently on one of her twice yearly diplomatic missions back to Sinotalya, and suddenly Dia wished heartily that both of his siblings were safely on the far side of the Cylbrin mountains with her.

"I won't get you involved in this. I'm sorry, but I just

won't. All I can do is promise you that I'll make sure that you and Rus stay safely out of it."

"Dia... It's not me and Rus I'm worried about." Their fingers tightened in the fabric of their skirt. "It's you. It always has been. Ever since father... I've been afraid you'll be next."

Dia's shoulders slumped. "I'm sorry." He said it again. What else could he say? He couldn't tell them not to worry or promise that he wouldn't get hurt, not when he could feel the queen's web tightening around him with every hour that passed.

Evren let out a soft breath. "Will you at least tell me who that man really is? You called him your friend but..."

The tension in Dia's shoulders eased slightly. This much reassurance, at least, he could give them. "It's a little bit complicated, but he really is a friend." It was true wasn't it? After last night Calix really was becoming a friend, the first Dia had had outside of his family since the Burning of Avarniy. The thought of Calix left an odd warmth in his chest, strange yet not unpleasant.

Evren studied him for a moment and then some of the tension seemed to leave their body as well. "Alright, even if you won't let me help, I'm glad that you're not doing whatever this is alone."

"So am I." Dia admitted it quietly as he lay back down against the cushions.

At those words a small smile flickered to life on Evren's lips. They watched him for another moment then got to their feet, smoothing down the dark blue fall of their skirt.

"It's my night in the clinic apothecary tonight but I don't have to be there 'til ten, so let me know if you need anything before that?"

Dia nodded. "Thanks Ev."

They turned away, back toward the house then paused for a moment and glanced back.

"For what it's worth, I still don't think what happened to father was your fault." Then, before Dia could answer, they strode away back up the path to the back door leaving the prince staring after them.

Half an hour later he was still staring at the closed door, still trying to come to terms with the tangle of emotions Evren had left him with when a falcon's call pulled him from his thoughts. Dia raised his head a little and saw that, sure enough, circling just beyond the bows shading him was the familiar gray and white form of Frost. Messenger birds were trained to return to the aviary but Dia's tended to be the exception. He had always had a way with them, especially with the more difficult birds like the White Peaks falcons, which were highly prized for their swift flight but so temperamental that they rarely made good messengers. The prince had raised several from chicks, including Frost, and they were all as likely to bring their messages straight to him as they were to bring them back to the aviary.

The falcon gave another irritated cry and Dia sat up, ignoring the slight spinning in the back of his head as he extended an arm. Frost dove for it and a moment later the prince felt the familiar impact followed by the equally familiar prick of talons as they pierced the dark purple fabric of his shirt. There was a letter tied to the falcon's leg and Dia smiled at the sight, thoughts momentarily diverted from his conversation with Evren. The seal was plain wax but he knew exactly who this must be from. Jamal.

Dia took a moment to stroke Frost's neck then pulled loose the cord holding the letter in place. His heart was beating faster now, and he had to admit to himself that it wasn't because of his illness. The sight of the myriad scars covering Calix's torso and arms flashed across his mind followed by a wave of guilt. With all Calix knew about Dia's secrets and weaknesses the act of investigating him should have felt like nothing but fair play, yet it did not, not after seeing those scars, not now that he realized that investigating Calix's past would likely also mean prying into the trauma and tragedy that had so marked him. Doing so felt like a violation of the precious trust growing between them, and yet... And yet Dia had not spent six years building a power base of knowledge and secrets to turn away from information now.

Ignoring the feeling of wrongness, Dia shifted Frost to the wooden perch he had erected beside the day bed several years earlier then, taking a quick breath, Dia unrolled the scroll.

He froze.

The letter was in the simple code of their childhood and the words came quickly to him, too quickly.

'Dia,

I did as you asked and spoke with Governor Moston about your royal guard. He does not exist. Neither Governor Moston nor any member of his household has ever met someone matching the description you gave me. I then made some inquiries in his hometown and among the Car Culond city guard. I found nothing. Whoever he is I can tell you this much: There is no evidence here that the man calling himself Calix Acalion existed before he appeared in Tar Mel.

Be careful.

Jamal.

For a long time Dia simply stared at the paper spread across his lap, the shock of his cousin's words radiating through him. He had thought that Calix might be the pawn of a member of Moston's family, or perhaps even a bastard of their blood, sent to Tar Mel to carry out their agenda or pursue his own, but this... This shouldn't have been possible. Calix had only been welcomed into the royal guard because of his letter of introduction, a letter sealed with the crest of house Moston. Had the crest been a perfect forgery? Or had Calix somehow found a way to steal the old man's seal?

Who was he?

If everything Dia knew of the Fox's past was a lie then who was he and what was his goal in Tar Mel? Why craft such an elaborate identity? Why go so far?

Dia's hands began to shake, his whole body turning cold, because it was obvious, so trickster cursed obvious. Calix claimed to come from Car Culond, from a city on the border with Estron. What if he came from the far side of the border? Dia was a fool. He had been so caught up in the politics of court that it never occurred to him Calix could be working for someone beyond the borders of H'arn. Yet now it all became perfectly clear. Pick a recluse lord to forge a letter of reference from, someone who could be counted on to not come to court and ruin the lie. Pick an area Calix was familiar with, somewhere he knew well enough to answer questions about. Make contacts among the servants and the other guards in order to find the secrets of the royal family. Hide in the garden to learn what the queen was meeting about. Cover for the prince when he was caught in order to blackmail him into revealing information. Foster a relationship with that prince in order to learn everything he could about the fissures within the royal family and the court and send all of that information back to his handlers in Estron.

Dia felt the paper crumpling beneath his fingers, felt

the peaceful memories of the previous night turning bitter on his tongue because there was only one explanation that made all the pieces fit.

Calix was an Estronian spy.

DIA FOUND Calix in the barracks. The guards playing dice outside of it had given him raised eyebrows and knowing looks when he asked for directions to Calix's room. Before Jamal's letter the sight of their ruse working so effectively would have amused him, but now it just made Dia feel cold. When he reached the door he didn't knock, just pushed it open, half hoping to catch Calix in the act of doing something illicit, and half hoping not to. Part of him still clung to the memory of the afternoon and evening, of Calix tackling the assassin to save him, of Calix saying that Dia had his support and his silence, but those memories only made the rest of him burn more, in pain, humiliation, betrayal. A spy. Calix was an Estronian spy. He had been using Dia from the beginning. It was so obvious and yet, caught up in court intrigue and, he had to admit now, his own loneliness, he hadn't seen it.

He would not make that mistake again.

When the door opened Calix's head snapped up. He had been lying on his bed reading, and his eyes widened at the sight of Dia even as he got quickly to his feet.

"Your Highness, it seems you're quite invested in spreading these rumors."

Before the letter Dia would have replied in kind, amused, irritated and challenged by whatever the Fox threw at him. Now though, he simply offered a small smile, his gaze flicking over the room, taking in the simple bed, the wardrobe, the desk. Other than leaving a short coat over the back of the desk chair and propping his rapier against the wall, Calix had done nothing to personalize the space.

"Actually I'm here about tonight."

"Oh?" Calix settled back onto the bed, studying him carefully. Dia looked steadily back, refusing to flinch or look away. He had spent years training himself to control his expression, his tone, his mannerisms, all the things that could so easily give him away. Now he called on those years of training, forcing himself to keep his expression open and honest, to keep his tone concerned but calm.

"There seems to have been some books missing from my original list. The librarian I know found that the queen often visits the library to read. She doesn't take the books out so they were not on the initial list but the librarian was able to figure out which ones she frequents. I want to try using those as the cipher before we do something dangerous like breaking into her rooms again."

"I see…" Calix studied him for a moment then nodded. "Alright. If that's what you want."

"It is." Dia tried for casual, but he heard a little bit of stiffness seeping into his tone. Calix must have heard it too because something sharpened in his gaze.

"We shouldn't wait too long though, unless you want your head to be on the block?"

"I know the stakes." Dia snapped, then, catching himself, "I just think this is the best way."

Calix shrugged with an affectation of carelessness which Dia no longer believed. "Whatever you say, Your Highness."

There was sarcasm in Calix's tone, a mocking lilt to Dia's title, a slight teasing curve of his lips.

Dia turned abruptly away, hands clenching at his sides. That look made Dia want to strike him, to shout at him, to strangle him, to spend another evening trading barbs with him. Yet Calix was an Estronian spy in the very heart of H'arn. Maybe his intentions toward Dia weren't entirely mercenary, maybe some of the trust and warmth Dia had begun to feel truly had been reciprocated. It hardly mattered. An enemy spy in his city was an enemy spy in his city. Destroying H'arn had been Estron's goal for two entire centuries, and Calix was a part of that. Whatever his own feelings, Dia needed to stay away from him if he didn't want to aid in his own kingdom's destruction. Realistically, he knew he should turn what he now knew over to the royal guard because every minute Calix walked freely through Tar Mel the danger he presented only increased, yet the Fox knew far too many of Dia's secrets to hand him over just like that. Besides, the idea of handing Calix over to the guard hurt Dia in a way he wasn't ready to explore, not now, not when he had so many other things to do—like finding a way to stop Calix from reporting what he knew back to his handlers and like sneaking into the queen's chambers to look at her books, something Dia would now be doing alone.

CHAPTER 9
THE PIPER

Dia waited for the sun to set before approaching the small wall gate. Except for the lanterns in their posts at the top of the wall the night was dark, fog rising to dim both moon and stars, making the towers of the Crown look like an eerie warning looming out of the gloom. Someone had changed the lock on the gate since Dia last entered. It was more sophisticated now, complex with extra tumblers. But it was forged by Malical, the best locksmith in all Tar Mel, and they had been three years now in Dia's debt. They were always happy to teach him the ins and outs of their work and happy, too, to give him samples to take apart to satisfy the prince's curiosity. If they suspected that he had other reasons for wanting a sample of every style of lock they created, well, they had so far kept any such suspicions to themself. Even in the dark, Dia's picks moved deftly within the lock and after a couple of minutes he was rewarded with the click of its release.

He slipped in through the gate, soft boots barely making a sound against the paving stones. On the far side the cobble stones became a winding path edged by trees and flowering bushes and in the middle of that garden courtyard stood his goal—the queen's chambers. Once, before the Palace City had been remodeled, with its underground network of flowing water for use and for sewage, the queen had lived within the Crown itself, as had all the rest of the royal family. But to live on anything above the first story was to live without the amenities that network of piping offered, so the greenhouses which once occupied these gardens had been taken down and new quarters had been built. The queen and her children occupied the ones to the left of the towers, Princess Emira the ones to the right, and the king the ones at the center just behind the towers themselves.

Dia had heard that some of the gardeners of the palace city mourned the loss of the gardens as they once were, but tonight Dia had no objections. Breaking into the Crown proper would have been much more difficult. As it was, as long as he got inside undetected he should be all right. Thanks to the same servant who had tipped him off about the queen's mysterious meeting several nights earlier, Dia knew that she had gone to join a strategy meeting the king was holding in the Crown proper. Apparently there was some scandal about it too. The king had been holding the meeting in secret and the queen was going to join uninvited. Ordinarily Dia would burn with curiosity to know what that was about, but tonight his mind was still churning over Jamal's letter and it was all he could do to focus on the task at hand.

Dia was only halfway down the winding path between the gate and the queen's quarters when it happened. There was the sound of movement ahead of him, a sense of shifting darkness, and then the spark and flaring of a lantern. In its sudden light Dia could see two figures standing beside the entrance of the queen's chambers. He froze, heart racing. There had never been guards posted inside the walls of the Crown before, certainly not to guard what should be an empty building. An instant later the realization dawned in him, as clear as it was obvious. This was because of him, because the queen knew that someone had gotten close enough to her chambers to spy on her. She had set a trap to catch anyone who should try such a thing again. He should have considered the possibility earlier but Calix had snuck into her rooms to copy the letter, and even when they were planning this attempt together he had not mentioned anything about additional guards. Had this been a set up all along? Had Calix meant for him to be caught?

"Who's there? Show yourself!" One of the guards snapped, brandishing their lantern.

Dia spun around, preparing to flee, but he had only gone a step before an answering lantern flashed out from within the garden, moving rapidly back in the direction of the gate. A thorough trap. He was going to be cut off. Wildly Dia spun around, scanning the darkness for any place to hide, any chance of escape. The guards by the queen's chambers were stepping closer now, lanterns held high. Dia's cloak hid his face for now, but it would do nothing if they caught him.

"Give up! There's nowhere to run!" One of the guards behind him called out. Dia didn't turn to look, his eyes still frantically scanning for anything that could save him. Maybe he could run through the garden, get them to chase him, then double back through the gate? Maybe...

A low hum fill the air around him, a melody. Dia's eyelids fluttered. He swayed slightly, sudden tiredness washing over him. ...What? Dia blinked rapidly, the sudden sensation taking him utterly off guard. When his eyes cleared again he saw that the guards had stopped moving, that they were dropping to the ground or leaning back against the trees, their whole bodies relaxing. Dia blinked again trying to make sense of what he was seeing, but with that soothing melody still running all around him it was hard to think.

... Melody? Music? Since when was there music?

The click of heels striking cobblestone broke through Dia's thoughts. He spun around in the direction of the wall gate then stilled, sure his mind must be playing tricks on him, sure he could not be seeing what he thought he was seeing.

Through the mist surrounding the gate walked a figure, his steps slow and deliberate as though nothing in the world could threaten him. In his hands was a slender pipe of pale wood, his fingers, long and clever, moving quickly over the stops. Around him three yellow gold balls of light illuminated his path and the guards line crumpled around him, their light catching on the orange of his hair and the gold of his eyes.

"Calix." Dia breathed the name as the Fox's gaze met his own. His mind felt blurry and oddly peaceful, too much so for the confusion and anger he knew he should feel. "What..."

Never raising his mouth from the pipe Calix nodded in the direction of the queen's chambers. For a moment Dia just stared at him dumbly, then realization struck and he turned, moving as quickly as his oddly relaxed body would allow, and pushed open the door, stepping inside. A moment later Calix followed and once the door was closed behind them he lowered his pipe.

The lack of the music left a strange ringing in Dia's ears.

He blinked, then blinked again, and then a third time, and with each blink the world seemed to grow clearer until he was staring at the Fox in utter shock because none of this was possible. Calix shouldn't be here, shouldn't have even known Dia was going to be here, but all of that paled in comparison to a much greater impossibility, the pipe. The magic, for magic it must have been. Dia had read about such things in old records and myths of the age before the Dragons' War. But this? To see something like this? Music, sound, used as a weapon? That was not how their magic worked. The gifts were born of cosmic energy, lightning and fire, light and heat, even the cursed gift of the killing void, all gifts of the cosmos, land of the gods. This though... This was something else entirely, a power which should no longer exist within the bounds of their world. The gates were closed, no one could enter or leave, and, besides, the stars circling Calix were proof that he was of their world, his gift a product of their reality. Unless...

"That's a relic isn't it?"

Dia pointed at the pipe.

Calix inclined his head and Dia drew in a quick breath, excitement lighting his eyes. He had read about these too, the relics, objects imbued with magics of other worlds in ways that were beyond the understanding of his people but which gave them a power independent of the user. Once, before the Crimson Age, before the Dragons' War, such objects had been, if not common then not quite rare either. Centuries of war and the sealing of the gates had changed all of that. Now the relics were nearly priceless, hidden away in the troves of kings or buried in the rubble of the lost lands or drowned beneath the sea. How did Calix come to have such a thing?

...Calix.

As reality caught up to him the light died from Dia's eyes and he took a quick step back, his tone cooling.

"What are you doing here?"

Calix gave him a measured look. "Saving your life, apparently."

Dia gritted his teeth. "I mean how are you here? We agreed on tomorrow night."

"We did." Calix stepped past him into the queen's study, the stars bobbing after him to illuminate the darkened room. "But none of that really sounded like you, so I decided to come anyway in case you happen to be lying."

Dia followed, stopping in the doorway and doing his best to sound cold and aloof, trying to hide the hurt bubbling just beneath his skin. "You know all about lying, don't you, Calix Acalion of Car Culond."

Calix, who had been starting to examine one of the queen's bookshelves, stiffened, then carefully placed his pipe on the queen's desk before slowly turning back to Dia, his face an empty mask.

"So that's what it is."

Dia crossed his arms. "That's what it is."

"You really do have quite the network don't you, Demiter?"

Dia glared at him. "You already knew I did. Did you think I wouldn't investigate you? Did you think I wouldn't figure it out?"

Calix looked away. "I thought it would take you longer." There was something new in his tone now, something Dia had never heard in it before, resignation, a strange ache which echoed in Dia's own heart. Calix wasn't supposed to sound like that. He was supposed to sound mockingly arrogant and unconcerned. He didn't get to sound resigned, to sound hurt and lonely when he was the one who had played on Dia's loneliness, the one who had caused the hurt.

"Longer to figure out what? That you lied about me having your support or about you being an Estronian spy?"

"I didn't lie about supporting you!" Calix's head snapped back up, his eyes wild.

"What about being a spy?" Dia took a step toward him. "Do you deny it?"

Calix glanced away again. "No but..."

"But what!"

"It's more complicated than you know!"

"Oh really? Then tell me!" Dia took two more steps forward until he was directly in front of Calix. "Tell me!"

Still the Fox refused to meet his eyes. "I can't tell you."

"Why not?"

"I can't tell you that either."

"Really?" Dia clenched his fists at his sides, struggling to keep from grabbing Calix and shaking him. "You've tricked, dragged, blackmailed and extorted my secrets out of me since the day we met, but you won't even tell me why you can't tell me?" His voice was shaking, his hands trembling. "After everything..."

"I can't!" Calix snapped the words, at last returning his gaze to Dia's, and the prince was shocked by the sudden haunted, aching look in those golden eyes. Calix took a couple of steps toward Dia then stopped, hands clenching and unclenching at his sides. "I can't tell you why I'm doing this! I can't tell you why I can't tell you! All I can tell you is that I'm not your enemy!"

"You want to drag my kingdom back into war!"

"I want peace!" Calix's voice cracked with the desperate volume of his shout, an odd empty little laugh followed it, tumbling from his lips to drop into the space between them. "If you believe nothing else I ever say, believe that I want peace."

Dia stared at him, momentarily speechless, the desperation in Calix's voice, the empty pain in his eyes, it was all so wrong and hurt and angry though he might be Dia, couldn't believe it was an act. No, this ran far deeper. This was real. Whatever this was, whatever Calix was really doing here, his hurt and despair were real.

"I..." Dia wasn't entirely sure what he was going to say but he didn't have a chance to find out because just then, from the front hall just beyond the study, came the unmistakable sound of the front door opening.

Instantly Dia and Calix's gazes locked, their fight forgotten in unifying panic. Then they were moving, Dia ducking back behind the half open study door even as Calix lunged back toward the desk and toward his pipe. He didn't make it. Queen Reanun Korvin stormed into the study, three guards on her heels, and froze.

"What in the Hexium!"

Calix reached for the pipe anyway only for his hand to snap back as something silver whipped through the air. A moment later a throwing knife landed in the wood of the desk just where the Fox's fingers would have been.

"Keep your hands where I can see them, thief."

The words came from the same source as the knife, a big balding man standing beside the queen, who Dia recognized as Ovrin Smyth, captain of the queen's personal guard.

Dia's heart was pounding, his breath coming too fast. What was the queen doing back so early? They should have had another hour. Had something happened to end the meeting early? Had the king denied her entry? It hardly mattered, because as Dia watched Smyth advance on Calix, alone and armed only with a dagger, a far colder realization coiled around Dia's heart.

Calix was going to die.

The Fox might be a skilled fighter but so were the queen's men. Outmatched, practically unarmed, and still recovering from his wound, Calix didn't stand a chance of escape, and Dia knew, with a sudden sick certainty, that the Fox would not be arrested either.

The queen had too many secrets, and she had no way of knowing what Calix had seen, what he knew.

She wouldn't take the risk.

She wouldn't let him leave her rooms alive.

She would capture him.

She would interrogate him.

She would get rid of him.

And that would be the end.

No one would question the queen, and she would have no reason to hesitate, not when Calix had no title, no power, not when his death held no consequences for her. And if it came out that he was an Estronian spy? Well, then she would not even have to hide what she had done. She would be lauded for it, for killing a traitor and protecting her kingdom.

Calix's fingers closed around the hilt of his dagger. Smyth raised another throwing knife. The two guards flanking him drew their swords.

"Your Highness." Dia stepped from the shadow of the doorway. "Forgive me for letting myself in. I was hoping to speak with you."

CHAPTER 10

MIDNIGHT

At the sound of his voice all heads whipped in Dia's direction, the shock obvious on their faces. It was the queen who recovered first. Reanun was a tall woman, pale skinned and pale haired with shrewd gray eyes which narrowed as they fixed on him.

"Prince Diamond. This is a surprise." She pushed between her guards to move directly in front of him, her eyes on a level with his.

Dia's heart was still racing and yet now that he had made his choice, now that there was no longer any going back, a strange sort of calm seemed to descend on him, allowing him to stare directly back into her eyes without flinching.

"May I take it you are the reason I found my guards asleep at their posts?"

"You may." He kept his entire attention fixed on the queen, not giving Calix so much as a glance. The queen was used to dealing with the nobility, treating the soldiers and servants who followed them as invisible extensions of their masters. If he failed to acknowledge Calix as an individual then hopefully so would she.

"I see…" The queen's eyes roved over him as though reassessing the potential threat. "And what do you want to say to me so urgently?"

Dia held her gaze, his voice calm and even, a hint of a smile even curving his lips.

"The assassin didn't die instantly."

Queen Reanun was a master of court intrigue and the control that came with it, so her expression only flickered, surprise showing just for a moment before it disappeared again behind a mask of calculation. Yet it had been there long enough for Dia to see it, for Dia to know that he had caught her off guard. Good. As long as he could keep her unbalanced this should work.

"Is that so?"

"It is and during his final moments we managed to *induce* him into signing a confession in his own blood documenting the orders you gave him. I don't think my father will be happy to hear that you were plotting to kill his heir, do you?"

The queen's brows drew together, narrowing into a dangerous line. "Do you really think it will be that easy? All I have to do is say you forged the confession. Without a living witness it's my word against yours, a desperate prince so bitter about being disinherited that he's willing to do anything for a taste of power."

Dia didn't flinch just smiled blandly back. "Maybe, but if anything should happen to me that would add credence to the confession don't you think?"

The queen took a step toward him. "Is that what you've come to tell me?"

Dia nodded. "It is. I have no interest in the feud

between you and Princess Emira. Do as you want, but if I disappear or am harmed in any way that confession will be delivered to my father."

The queen's eyes narrowed. "That will be cold comfort to you in your grave, prince."

Dia met her gaze steadily. "Maybe, but would the knowledge that you had put me in my grave be enough to comfort you in your own?"

Their gazes locked for a moment and then Dia turned abruptly on his heel. "Good night, your majesty."

With that, he pushed past the stunned guards and strode from the room, not hesitating or looking back, relying only on the sound of heels clicking against floorboards to tell him that Calix was behind him. Even once they reached the garden Dia forced himself to keep his head held high and his stride measured, ignoring the instincts screaming at him to run. When they reached the wall gate Calix caught up with him, falling into step beside him without a word. They continued like that until they reached Dia's home and he had shut the door of his bedroom behind them. Then, at last, Dia let go of his control and sank shaking down the wall to the floor beside the door.

"She's going to try to kill you." It was Calix who spoke first, dark certainty in his voice.

"I know." Dia said it quietly, and he did know, his whole body shaking with the knowledge. In front of the queen he had been calm and in control, but now, safely hidden in the darkness of his room, the terrifying realization of what he had done was rising up to drown him. Before he had been a target but only a minor threat, already disowned and without an obvious faction at court. The queen had seen him more as a means to removing Emira then an ends in himself. Calix had been right, before this: if he had thought there was truly no way out, he could always have taken his siblings and fled to his mother's kin. Now though... Now he was a threat to her, now he would have to be removed. Most likely there would be an assassin, one who would torture Dia for the whereabouts of the supposed documentation before killing him in a way that would frame anyone other than the queen. He already knew that Queen Reanun knew where to find assassins. Giving such orders would not take her long.

"I won't let her." There was sharp determination in Calix's voice as he dropped to kneel beside Dia, the stars flickering up from his palm to cast a dim golden light over the otherwise darkened room.

Dia shook his head. "You should run, get out of the city. Otherwise she'll just kill you too."

"You saved my life. I'm not going to run and leave you to die."

A hollow laugh slipped from between Dia's lips, born of the panic still coursing through him, turning his breath to shuttering gasps.

"I thought you hated Demiters."

"I do, I just don't hate you." Calix grabbed Dia's wrists, whether to force him to listen or to emphasize the sincerity of his words Dia didn't know, but the touch sent a shock through the prince's skin, beating back the panic to ground him in his body. It was strange. Barely an hour before Dia had been furious with Calix and now his touch felt like the only thing keeping the prince afloat.

Calix.

"What's your name?" The question slipped from Dia's lips before he could think better of it.

"What?" The Fox started at the question but to Dia's relief he didn't let go.

"Is it really Calix?"

The Fox tensed, his eyes searching Dia's face as though trying urgently to solve a puzzle written there. "It's not the name my parents gave me, but it is the one I chose, if that's what you're asking?"

Dia nodded and he felt Calix relax again. There was silence for a moment as they just stared at each other, Dia focusing everything he could on the feel of Calix's hands on his wrists, grounding him against the tide of panic still churning in his blood, the reality that he was dead.

It was Calix who moved first, hands loosening on Dia's wrists then beginning to pull away.

"Don't! Don't let go!" Dia's words, quiet and desperate, were out before he could call them back, and in his panicked need to keep contact he actually lunged forward to grab Calix's forearms.

Calix stilled, his own eyes widening. "And there I thought you hated me for being an Estronian spy."

"I…" Dia struggled, unable to put words to the emotions churning deep within him. "I don't hate you. I just… You're an agent of Estron, my kingdom's enemy…"

"I'm not *your* enemy." Calix's voice was low and intense, causing something to spark and jitter deep within Dia's chest.

"Then what are you?" Dia's voice was hoarse, his head spinning with panic and with something else, the deep urgent need to escape the panic if only for a moment.

Calix leaned closer, a challenge gleaming in his golden eyes. "What do you want me to be?"

Dia's heart stuttered. Calix's face was so close, his eyes which seemed to glow in the light of his magic, the orange sweep of his lashes, his lips… A sudden sense-memory returned to Dia, Calix's body pressing him against one of the pillars of the aviary, his mouth soft against Dia's own. At the time he had thought little of it, the experience utterly drowned out by everything else that had happened that night, but now... Now that Dia knew Calix, now that his proximity, his touch, was the only thing keeping Dia grounded amid the storm of panic threatening to engulf him, the need to answer the challenge in Calix's eyes, to feel those lips against his own again, rose up quick and hot in him. Before he had a chance to think it through Dia found himself closing the distance between them to capture Calix's lips in a desperate kiss.

CHAPTER 11
BURNING

Calix responded instantly, his mouth equally desperate against Dia's own. He tugged his arms free of Dia's grip and wrapped them around the prince's neck, pulling him closer. Dia went willingly, leaning in, his own arms wrapping around the Fox's back, hands finding purchase in the fabric at the back of his jacket. The kiss was urgent and clumsy and sent a wave of new sensations through Dia washing his mind clean of thoughts until, for a few moments, there was nothing but sensation; the taste of Calix's mouth, the brush of his tongue over Dia's lips, the feel of fingers tangling in his hair...

At last it was the need for air which forced them apart and for a moment they just stared at each other panting softly. Then Calix leaned in again, so close that Dia could feel the Fox's breath against his lips.

"Don't give up yet, Your Highness. We will find a way through this." Calix's voice was low and warm, and it sent a shudder down Dia's spine.

"You don't need to keep calling me that. Just Dia is fine."

"Dia." Calix repeated, his lips curving around the name, and there was something almost familiar about how he said it, something that felt like an echo of a memory. Then Calix was kissing Dia again, slower and more lingering, and Dia found himself once again lost in sensation.

When the kiss broke for the second time Calix untangled one of his hands from where it had been making a mess of Dia's braid to cup the side of the prince's jaw, thumb running lightly across his cheek. "Better now?"

Dia nodded, leaning into Calix's touch. The panic was still there but more remote now, tamped down by other, warmer emotions.

"No more telling me to run and save myself?"

"You should still run."

Calix's eyes narrowed. "I told you I'm not going to just leave you to die."

"Stubborn fox." The words were out of Dia's mouth before he had a chance to think them through.

Calix started, his eyes widening. "What did you call me?"

"I... Nothing." Dia's tongue nearly stumbled over the denial in his haste to get it out, his cheeks turning pink as he realized that this was the first time he'd used his private nickname for Calix out loud. Hurrying to distract him he kept going. "Besides, we don't have a chance against the queen. We didn't even get to look at her books so we aren't any closer to deciphering that letter."

"I saw the titles on some of them."

Dia started back in surprise. "Do you remember any of them?"

Calix nodded. "She had an almost complete set of the Hexium."

Dia shook his head, his shoulders slumping. "I tried them already when I was trying random common books on the cipher."

He expected to see equal disappointment in the Fox's eyes, but instead Calix just looked like he was thinking. "I don't think these were the standard additions. They had a date seal on the bottom of the spines from nearly a hundred years ago. Wasn't that before the latest volume configuration?"

Dia's eyes widened. Then he was detangling himself from Calix so that he could push himself to his feet and rush for his own bookcases, hands moving over spines as he peered through the dimness at the titles, searching for the ones he wanted. Behind him he could hear Calix's heels clicking on the floorboards and a moment later there was a flare of light as the Fox lit the lamp on Dia's desk. In its glow Dia saw the books he was looking for, seven volumes bound in crimson and stamped in gold. The first six were each dedicated to one of the six gods of the Hexium, the deities said to rule over the divine realm. The seventh, the Book of the Devine, was an encyclopedia of all the gods, major and minor, that were known to be worshiped throughout their world. Beside them sat another set. That one, bound in black and gold, was the modern set found in every library and many private homes, but Dia was a scholar whose fascination with the evolution of their world since the ending of the Dragons' War had been more than a mere cover story. He possessed both the modern edition and the previous one, it's different configuration, and the additional stories and annotations added in the newer version, giving it a different layout of chapter and page, a layout he had not yet tried to insert into the cipher.

Quickly Dia began pulling the crimson volumes from the shelf, glancing over his shoulder as he asked, "You said *almost* a complete set? Which volumes were missing?"

"The Star Fox." Calix's lips twisted in an ironic smile. "It appears a queen plotting a coup has very little use for a god of peace."

Dia nodded and pushed the volume back onto the shelf before carrying three others over to his desk. Calix scooped up the other three and followed, adding them to the stack. Dia dropped into his seat and pulled the queen's letter toward himself, beginning to flip through the pages as Calix once again perched on the corner of Dia's desk. This time Dia found his proximity oddly distracting, the taste of Calix's lips still so fresh on his own, but he did his best to push the thoughts away. Whatever heat had possessed him in that moment of panic and despair, whatever tangled emotions he still felt clinging between them, he would have time to unravel them later—after he found out if this last gambit was going to pay off.

It didn't.

As the clock in the top of the Crown chimed out midnight Dia pushed the final book aside, his shoulders slumping.

"It's not any of these."

Calix let out a disappointed huff of breath, fingers drumming against the wood of Dia's desk. "Perhaps I should take another look at her bookshelves."

"No!" Dia sat back in his chair so fast that it made his head spin, but he ignored the sensation glaring up at Calix. "You almost died the last time you went in there and now you want to go back?"

Calix slipped a hand into his short coat and pulled out his pipe, which he must have retrieved from the queen's desk while she and her guards were focused on Dia. "I have my ways, remember?" His lips quirked teasingly as he said it, as though tempting Dia into an argument which would end in the prince letting him go. Dia didn't rise to the bait, instead his eyes sliding past Calix to rest on the one crimson volume remaining on his bookshelf.

"What if you don't need to?"

"Oh?" Calix arched an eyebrow at him.

In answer Dia stood, moving to the bookshelf and pulling the remaining volume from it.

"What if the reason the collection is incomplete isn't because the queen isn't interested in a god of peace? What if it's because she keeps that volume somewhere else, somewhere closer to hand in a desk drawer or by her bedside in case she needs it?"

Calix's eyes widened at that but he said nothing, just watched as Dia pulled the volume from the shelf and returned to his desk, beginning to flip through it. A few moments later Dia gasped, excitement lighting in his pale gray eyes.

"I think this is it! I'm getting an actual sentence this time!"

"... Of course it would be that book."

Dia started at the words. He had expected Calix to share in his excitement but instead there was only bitterness in the Fox's tone. Glancing up, Dia found the same bitterness reflected in the Fox's face.

"Do you have something against the god of peace?"

The Fox gave him a look dripping in an irony Dia couldn't fathom.

"Don't you?"

Dia blinked. "Why would I?"

Calix gestured to the world around them. "We are living through a time so drenched in blood and war that we named it the Crimson Age. It's been two hundred years and the god of peace has done nothing to save anyone. No matter how hard people pray he only abandons the world. Why wouldn't I despise him?"

Dia stared at Calix for a long moment, utterly at a loss for words. He wasn't personally a follower of the Star Fox, at least not specifically, but he did pray to him sometimes like he did all the other gods of the Hexium. Even if there was never an obvious answer to his prayers, it wasn't like he truly expected one. That wasn't really how gods worked after all. Sometimes they sent dreams and sometimes the weather changed, but descending from the divine realm to stop wars with their own hands was simply not a thing they did. Still, there was so much bitterness in Calix's voice that Dia didn't want to simply brush his words aside. Not sure what else to do, he only nodded and turned his attention back to his decryption.

Minutes passed in silence as Dia worked and, slowly, as the time ticked by, the prince felt his excitement turned to confusion and then to dread. At last he stopped, staring at the mostly decoded message before him, unable to go on.

Calix must have noticed when the scratching of Dia's pen fell silent because he glanced up, peering over the prince's shoulder to try to get a look at the decrypted letter.

"What is it?" The Fox must have noticed the new alarm in Dia's posture because there was tension in his voice.

"We were wrong." In contrast Dia's voice was empty, shock and horror leaching the intonation from it.

"It isn't about the queen's plot?"

Numbly Dia shook his head. "No. It's about the king's."

"What!" Calix stiffened. "What plot?"

"His plot for Nomenie." Nomenie was the kingdom to H'arn's northwest. Smaller and less militarily inclined than the nations surrounding it, it maintained its independence through clever trade agreements and pitting the other regional powers against each other. Nomenie's mountain ranges were the richest source of iron and other critical metals on the continent and so Nomenie defended itself by ensuring that any nation which tried to invade them would be instantly set upon by every other nation in the area, none of which wanted any of their rivals to gain total control of Nomenie's mines.

That was, until now.

In hindsight, Dia realized, the signs had been there. For weeks now there had been rumors of a new assault against Estron yet no one had known exactly where it was going to be or the plan behind it. They only knew that troops were being mobilized. The crafters' workshops had been busy at all hours with the development and building of new mounts and rotating platforms for Yingtian's fire powder weapons, each shipment leaving the city just as soon as it was completed. Jamal had mentioned in one of his most recent letters to Dia the strange way in which his commander had reorganized their troops, as though, the prince now realized, to cover gaps farther along the border where other troops were being secretly withdrawn. Then there was the strategy meeting the queen had interrupted only that night, a strategy meeting so secret that even the queen wasn't supposed to know about it.

"The king is planning a secret invasion of Nomenie." Dia's voice was hollow as he stared at the paper before him, willing the words written on it to change. They did not, and so he continued. "He plans for it to be fast and brutal, so that there won't be time for any other nations to come to its defense. The Warlord of the West will be leading it, which is why she knows about it and why she wrote her sister. Apparently everything has been compartmentalized to keep Nomenie in the dark, but the invasion is imminent and will begin as soon as the king gives the order."

Dia finally raised his head, turning to Calix and finding his own horror reflected back at him in the Fox's gaze.

"It's going to be the Burning of Avarniy all over again."

CHAPTER 12

FATHER

"If I had to name the single biggest barrier between the Warlord of the West and the throne of H'arn it would probably be the Duchy of Yingtian. The Duchy was founded a century ago by a group of Zheng people fleeing the chaos and horrors that the Crimson Age brought to their own northeastern continent. Originally it was a part of Estron's territory which the King of Estron gave them in return for the Zheng craft masters using their advanced metal techniques to forge weapons for Estron. They gave him quite the edge in the war, yet he didn't value them nearly as much as he should have. He and his successor attempted to tax them into poverty to make them reliant on Estronian government contracts to pay those taxes, effectively indenturing them to the throne. The Zheng called his bluff. Rather than pay the taxes they put that money toward producing as many of their more advanced fire powder weapons as possible and in 164PC declared their independence, immediately signing a trade agreement with H'arn. It was a brilliant move but one that still left them in danger of some counter stroke by Estron. So, in summer 175PC the Duchess's daughter, Su Yin married, King Harlin Amarth Demiter of

H'arn, consolidating their position as a semiautonomous duchy within Estron's sphere of protection, and that is where the problems of Queen Reanun truly begin. Emira, granddaughter of the Duchess of Yingtian, is the only heir to the throne of H'arn that the people of Yingtian will accept. The Zheng have already proven themselves willing to rebel and they have the money and the technology to back up that willingness. For that reason, no matter what attempts the queen made to persuade my father to name one of her children is heir, there was no chance he would ever listen. He needs the Zheng's support too badly. For that reason also, the queen must make sure that Emira's death can never be traced back to her or her sister, for should the Duchess of Yingtian and the Warlord of the West clash, H'arn would fall to civil war."

-From the writings of Prince Diamond Havoran Demiter

"We have to stop him!" Calix was off of Dia's desk and on his feet in an instant.

"We do." Dia turned in his chair to watch as Calix began to pace the room, his own stomach was churning, fear and horror welling up to leach away all of the calm he had regained. "But I don't know how."

"There has to be something!" Calix snapped, raising his head to glare at Dia as though the prince had suggested doing nothing. "You said you wanted to be king to stop this from happening again!"

Dia raised his hands defensively. "I did and I do but I'm *not* king so it's not going to be that easy."

Calix's eyes narrowed. "You're just giving up?"

Dia stood, glaring back. "Of course not! I just said it wasn't going to be easy, that's all!"

They glared at each other for a moment only to be interrupted by the sound of a knock against the front door. Both men froze, anger turning to alarm in their eyes.

"I take it you weren't expecting guests at this hour?"

Wordlessly, Dia shook his head.

"Then don't answer it."

Dia shook his head again. "I have to. If they keep knocking like that they'll wake Ruslan or Hazan and I don't want either of them answering it."

Calix hesitated for a moment, then nodded.

"Do you have a sword?"

"Yes, but I'm no soldier."

"Give it to me then."

Dia nodded and reached into his wardrobe, pulling out a simple short sword and handing it to Calix. The Fox hefted it in his hand, testing the weight. The knocking came again. Calix pulled his pipe from his jacket with his free hand then nodded. "Let's go meet your guest."

Dia slowly eased the front door open, free hand on his dagger, Calix just behind him, ready and waiting for an attack. It didn't come. There was only one man standing on Dia's doorstep but the sight of him did nothing to calm the prince. It was Ovrin Smyth, captain of the queen's guard.

"Captain Smyth, to what do I owe the visit?"

"Prince." There was a smile on the captain's face that Dia didn't like. "Where is your sibling?"

Dia's eyes narrowed. "Which sibling." He had an awful sinking feeling he knew exactly who Smyth meant, but he didn't feel the need to give the man anything.

"Evren. They're an apprentice apothecary aren't they? That means they spend one night a week on call in the clinic, and would you talk about luck? Tonight just happens to be that night doesn't it?"

Dia tensed, fear and fury warring in him. "What do you

want?" Dia forced the words out from between gritted teeth.

Smyth smiled back in a way that made Dia want to strike him.

"I bring a message from my queen. Kill Princess Emira."

Dia's eyes widened. "Just like that?"

"Just like that. Do it before Evren's shift ends at noon or there is no telling what might happen." Smyth inclined his head in an exaggerated gesture of respect. "Good night, Prince." He turned away leaving Dia staring after him, his heart racing and dread coiling in his stomach.

Not again.

Not again.

Not...

A grave, a coffin, the sound of children weeping, the feel of his own body shaking, the sight of his mother's tears...

Not again.

Not Evren.

Not...

A warm hand descended on his shoulder, cutting through the tumult of his mind.

"Breath, Dia."

Dia took a shuddering breath.

"I have to save them."

"I know."

"I know we have to figure out how to stop the king from invading Nomenie ..."

"I understand." There was an ache in the Fox's voice, the pain of an old wound never quite healed. "If I had a chance to save my siblings there's nothing I wouldn't do."

Dia turned to look at him, surprised, as much by Calix volunteering information about himself as by anything else. "You have siblings?"

A bitter smile curved the corners of the Fox's lips. "I did."

*Oh...*Dia's tone softened. "I'm sorry."

"A lot of people are." There was something in the way Calix said it which made Dia uncomfortably sure that those people had become sorry on the edge of Calix's blade. "It doesn't bring them back. So I understand. I will help you save Evren, but as soon as it's done I will prevent the massacre of Nomenie by *any* means."

There was a threat somewhere in those words. Dia could hear it, but whatever it was he couldn't focus on it right now, not with Evren...

In a moment of rage and frustration Dia slammed the front door shut then strode across the darkened entrance hall to the bench and dropped onto it.

"I thought she was coming after me. I should have realized..."

"We both should have." Calix began pacing the entrance hall, the lights of the stars flickering up to hover about his head, lighting his path. "But I admit I didn't think she'd make a move this openly. It could be her undoing."

Dia shook his head, mind already churning with possibilities. "No, I don't think it will be. Smyth was right about them getting lucky. I bet Ev doesn't even know they're a hostage. That way if I go to my father and tell him, they can be brought in unharmed with no knowledge of what's happening, making it seem like I made the whole thing up. It would be worth it though. Even if it destroys my credibility, if I can save Ev..."

"Don't be too quick to assume they'd be safe. That's the trouble with you having two siblings you're known to love. A few days from now one of them could have an 'accident' and it would still leave the queen with a life to hold over your head."

"Trickster!" Dia spat the curse, his hands clenching and unclenching. He knew Calix was right and he hated it, hated that he had put his family in danger *again*. First his stepfather and now...

"Then we have to get Ev out of there."

Calix nodded and paused in his pacing to turn back to Dia, lightly waving his pipe at him.

"What about the direct approach?"

Dia stared for a moment then nodded slowly, hope sparking in him. Even if they completely ignored consequences and subtlety and tried to fight their way in, the queen probably had someone close enough to Evren to kill them before they could be rescued. But if everyone in the clinic, guards included, just happened to be asleep...

"When you used it in the garden I felt it but it didn't knock me out the way it did the guards. Was that your doing?"

Calix nodded. "It isn't perfect but I have some control."

On another night Dia would have been fascinated by that, would have had a dozen follow-up questions about how it worked, would have asked if he could try it for himself, but tonight he only nodded.

"Alright, then let's go."

THE CLINIC WAS on the western side of the Palace City, a large many branched building with stone walls and a roof of slanting gray slate. There was a garden surrounding most of it, combining the need for fresh healing herbs with a place those recovering from illness or injury might sit or walk as they healed. It had two entrances, the main one at the front of the building and a second one in back for supply deliveries. They decided to attempt to go in through the back, hoping that doing so would lead them into the areas of the clinic off-limits to patients, including, presumably, the room where on-call apprentices slept.

Dia and Calix stood in the alley between two houses, as close to the apothecary as they could get without stepping out into the open, and peered through the darkness.

"Two guards." Dia murmured.

Calix nodded. "I see them but they won't be seeing anything for long."

In the darkness the prince couldn't see Calix's face but he could still hear the smile in the Fox's voice as he lifted his pipe to his lips and began to play.

The music was beautiful, that was Dia's first thought—high and fair and otherworldly in some way he couldn't name. It melted with the air and the breeze, calming and soothing him. Making his eyelids flutter. Maybe that was why it took him so long to realize that nothing else was happening, the guards remaining unmoving at their posts. Then the song of Calix's pipe cut off abruptly and alarm crashed in, wiping the music's calm from Dia.

"What went wrong? Were they to far away?"

Calix shook his head, his voice a hiss of frustration. "No. They're in range. Those trickster-cursed guards from earlier must have remembered hearing music before they collapsed. They must have wax or something in their ears."

"Curses!" Dia's hands curled into fists. They had been so close, Evren so close and now... "I won't lose them."

"We need another way in." Calix peered out of the alley as though trying to assess the apothecary's possible weak points.

"No," Dia shook his head. "The queen isn't that sloppy. Any entrance is going to be guarded." His heart was beginning to pound, a last desperate idea forming in his mind. "If we're going to get inside we'll need help from someone the guards aren't watching for, someone who has just as much to lose from all of this as I do."

"Who?"

Dia turned on his heel so that he faced, not the clinic, but the towers of the Crown where they loomed above him.

"Princess Emira."

"I thought you didn't trust each other." Between the night and the shadows it was too dark for Dia to see the widening of Calix's eyes, but he could hear it in the surprise clinging to every word.

"We don't."

"Then what makes you think she'll listen to you now?"

"Nothing." As he spoke Dia began striding toward the Crown, not pausing to see if Calix would follow. "I barely know her. She's never been interested in a relationship and she plays everything so close to the chest that not even the servants I've bribed have been able to tell me much."

"Then... Dia wait. You have no evidence, no relationship with her, and you're just going to hope you can convince her?"

"Do you have a better plan?" Dia demanded. He could hear the unusual sharpness in his tone but he didn't apologize. He could apologize later. Once Evern was safe.

"I might, if you'd give me a moment to think about it." There was a slight edge now to Calix's voice too. "At least try to come up with something that doesn't risk your life too!"

"That doesn't matter anymore." Dia sped up until he was nearly running, as though if he moved fast enough he could somehow outpace this, as though this time, this time…

Calix's hand on the back of the prince's shoulder pulled him to an abrupt halt.

"Wait!" The Fox's voice was gentler now. "I get it but…"

"You don't though!" Dia spun to face him.

Calix jerked his hand back as though he had been burned, the light of a nearby lantern reflecting off of his flashing eyes.

"Don't I?" There was real anger now in the Fox's voice, and Dia winced, the memory of what Calix had told him about his own siblings cutting through the prince's desperate fury.

"Sorry." Dia took a shuddering breath, "I didn't mean it like that."

"Didn't you?" The old coolness was back in Calix's voice.

Dia shook his head. He hesitated for a moment, loath to take this time when every instinct still screamed for him to race for Evren's side, but if he stood any chance of protecting them then he needed Calix.

"I was fifteen when I first started plotting to take the throne. I was young and angry and I…" The words burned like bile in his throat. "I made mistakes."

Calix said nothing but Dia could see the surprise in his face, see the way his posture changed, relaxing slightly, listening.

"My mother's husband might not have been the man who sired me but he was my father in every way that mattered and I trusted him completely. He was also a general in the king's army. I told him what really happened in Avarniy and that I wanted the throne. I thought that, as a general, he could build support for me in the army."

"And he betrayed you?" Calix asked.

"No!" Dia snapped then caught himself, forcing his tone to soften. "Sorry. I know why you're asking. I know how it often is between parents and their step children, but no. My father really did love me and he really was a good man."

I wish he had betrayed me. I wish...

"He promised me his full support, but we weren't careful enough. *I* wasn't careful enough. I was too angry, too young..."

"What happened?" Calix asked the question gently.

"My *other* father found out." The words were bitter on Dia's tongue, bitter with a hatred that ran *so* much deeper than their shared blood. "He told me Emira was his heir, that he didn't appreciate being undermined, that he understood that I was young enough to make mistakes but that I still couldn't be allowed to forget my place like that, that I needed to be taught a *lesson*." Dia felt a sudden lump rising in his throat and had to quickly swallow it back down before finishing quietly. "He sent my father to the front line, to the battle of Mi Lor..."

There was no need for him to continue, he could see it in Calix's eyes, see that the Fox had figured out the rest. He knew there had always been questions about why King Harlin, who was known for being a cunning military man, had insisted on trying to defend Mi Lor. The order had been given for as many civilians as possible to evacuate and the king's advisers had all urged him to abandon the city completely. No one had ever known why he refused. No one had ever known why he sent one of his best generals to try to hold the city even after the loss of the land directly to its north and south had left it indefensible. No one had ever known why he had given his general so few troops.

No one, except Dia.

"I was supposed to have stopped then, but I didn't. I kept everything as close to my chest as I could. I wouldn't let anyone else in the family help, wouldn't tell them anything. I changed my tactics to influencing things at lower levels, levels that were below that man's notice. I couldn't let him keep total control of the kingdom, not after everything. I thought if I kept them all out of it I could keep them safe..." Dia's voice trailed away, mingled anger and self-reproach rising up to choke him.

A hand came to rest gently on his shoulder and this time Dia didn't shrug it away.

"We won't let anything happen to Evren."

Dia took a shuddering breath, gathering himself, and nodded. "No matter what it takes."

This time when Dia turned and began striding again toward the Crown, Calix was at his side.

CHAPTER 13

THE SERPENT

"*Despite what the rumors say, it truly was a cordial arrangement. Queen Su Yin understood that my father needed an heir, so when the doctors told her that she was unlikely to become pregnant she agreed with my father's other advisors. As for my mother, I have heard it said that my father demanded his way into her bed, but that isn't true either. He wooed her, always with the open honesty that she would never be queen; that's the other thing that so many people forget. My father loved Queen Su Yin and at one point he also loved my mother. Yet as it turns out the doctors were both right and wrong. Wrong because Queen Su Yin could conceive, and did so a little over a year after I was born; right, because she did not have the health to survive it.*

As a child, I never resented my father for disinheriting me. Emira was the daughter of his queen, so by all rights she must be heir. Yet I was two years older than her, so in order to grant her her birthright something needed to be done about me. The duchy played into it too, of course. They would never accept an heir other than Emira, which is why my father could not marry my mother after Queen Su Yin died. Doing so would have legit-

imized me. I suppose I would have resented it back then, when I was too young to understand political expedience, but my father left me to my mother to raise, and when she married my stepfather he treated me as though I was his own, and so, I was happy."

-From the writings of Prince Diamond Havoran Demiter

DIA HAD NEVER BEEN inside the gardens on the right side of the Crown before. For his entire life they had been the domain of the late Queen, Su Yin, and then that of her daughter, Emira. Dia had only been two when Queen Su Yin died and he did not remember her. As for Emira, their separate childhoods—his in his mother's house—hers in the crown, had naturally separated them, and it was a gap neither had ever sought to bridge.

There were guards at the entrance to Emira's quarters and, despite the lateness of the hour, they must have been on high alert because they moved the moment Dia and Calix came around the bend in the path.

"Intruder!" One of the guards raised her hand, flames leaping up from her palm. The other drew her blade.

"Not an intruder." Dia straightened his shoulders and pushed back his hood, watching the guards stiffen as firelight flickered across his face.

"Prince Diamond?" It was the one with the sword who spoke. She did not lower her blade.

Dia inclined his head in acknowledgment. "I need to speak with Princess Emira."

"At this hour?" It was the one with the flames in her hand who spoke, her dark eyes narrowing. "Anything you have to say can wait till morning." Behind him Dia felt Calix step closer, tension radiating off of him.

"No it can't." Dia took another step toward the guards, fear for Evren sharpening his tone until he could hear his father echoing within it. Normally he would have been uncomfortable with the comparison but right now he would use it. "Do you think I would be here at this hour if the matter wasn't urgent?"

"Her Highness is asleep." The guard with the sword tried.

"Then wake her!" Dia stepped forward again until the tip of her blade brushed against his chest. "I don't care if she's ill or in bed with a lover. I *will* see my sister!"

Sister. The word tasted wrong on Dia's lips. He had no sister. Emira was not his family, not in his mind or his heart, but in his blood, the blood they shared, that was a different story. He was the disinherited prince, the recluse, the scholar. Dia was close enough now to see the shock in the eyes of both guards as they were reminded of what so much of the court seemed to forget. He was also the elder brother of their princess and the firstborn child of their king. For a moment they just stared at him, then the one holding the sword hastily lowered her weapon and the one with the flames in her hand inclined her head.

"Very well Your Highness, this way."

The guards left them in what must be the princess's receiving room, its furnishings simple but elegant, its carpets woven in cream flecked through with patterns of gold, it's walls decorated with framed paintings of flowers, each done in so much detail that they appeared as much scientific study as art. They waited in silence, unwilling to give away anything to the guards who, Dia knew, must be standing just on the other side of the closed door. Calix kept his eyes fixed on it, tension in every line of his usually relaxed form. For his part it was all Dia could do to stay in his seat, the need to run to Evren's side nearly unbearable. Yet he knew he had to bear it, knew that this was the only way.

The princess kept them waiting for nearly half an hour. It was a power move, Dia was sure, a reminder that she was the superior in rank and did not come when he called, that his time was hers to spend, not the other way around. Normally it would not have fazed him. He was used to the subtle jibes and power plays of the court and it was nothing he couldn't ignore. Now though, with his sibling in danger, it was all he could do to fight back his frustration when Princess Emira finally stepped into the room.

She had taken the time to dress, another subtle display of power. Her gown was white and pale green, long and belted at the waist, the skirt cut straight and loose to keep from impeding her movements. Her black hair hung long and straight to her waist, unconfined except by the thin golden circlet which ringed her brows, another, far less subtle reminder of their relative positions. Behind Emira was Captain Omdare, fully dressed and fully armed, her expression every bit as cold as her princess's.

"Prince Diamond, to what do I owe the visit?"

Dia rose at her entrance, inclining his head, and a moment later, Calix did the same.

"Princess, I'm here to tell you the truth about the assassin."

Emira's expression didn't so much as flicker, her voice remaining coolly neutral. "He's an assassin now? I thought he was a bandit who attacked us randomly."

"I lied."

"Why? Was he your assassin?" Even as she asked the question Emira's tone still didn't change.

"No."

"Then why not tell me the truth?"

"Because I wasn't sure you would believe me if I told you who hired him."

The princess said nothing to that, only continued to watch him. Dia's eyes flickered across her face, searching for some sign of reaction or emotion, something that would guide his words, but still, nothing.

"This may be hard for you to hear, but the truth is that the queen is trying to kill you."

"I know."

Dia stiffened, his eyes widening. "What?"

"I said I know."

"But how?" Dia stared at her in utter shock. Out of every way he had imagined her reacting, it hadn't been like this. How could she have known? How could she possibly... "There wasn't anyone else in the garden that night. No one else could have overheard..."

"What garden?"

"The queen's garden, six nights ago."

Emira stared at him for a long moment, and then she did the last thing he had expected. She laughed. It wasn't a humorous laugh, nor was it a particularly cruel one, but it was a harsh sound nonetheless, filled with irony and a bitterness Dia did not understand.

"What is it?" As he asked his eyes flicked from the princess to her captain. Captain Omdare was watching him with narrow eyed appraisal that was far easier to read than Emira's cool mask, but if she was at all shocked by her princess's reactions her expression didn't show it.

Emira took a step toward Dia, emotion at last showing itself across her features as her lips quirked upward into a small, slightly bitter, smile. "Prince, my stepmother has been trying to kill me for years."

"What?" The word left Dia's mouth in a quiet gasp and he realized it was the third time he'd said it in as many minutes. He had been thrown by Emira's reactions and now he had completely lost control of the conversation. He needed to collect himself. For Evren's sake...

"Mmm..." Emira crossed her arms her eyes running across his features, searching for the lie in his reaction.

Dia took a breath, gathering himself, and began to feel out the implications of her words. Now that the first shock was passing he realized that it made perfect sense. Princess Castela's sixteenth birthday was the deadline pushing the queen to assassination, yet birthdays didn't come out of nowhere. The queen would have had years to plot and plan other ways to get rid of Emira, accidents and missteps that could be attributed to nothing more than bad fortune. In contrast, hiring an assassin and framing a prince was a risky move, a desperate move, and the queen *was* desperate, that much Dia saw now. Taking Evren hostage, even in such a subtle way, was the move of someone out of time and out of options, the move of someone trying to brute force a problem because subtlety had failed. He should have seen it then, should have realized she would only try something so rash if she had already exhausted her other options, but he had been too terrified for Evren to see it.

"If you've known about the issue then why haven't you done something about it?" Calix's familiar, slightly mocking tones, cut through Dia's thoughts. There was no deference in the question, none of the respect that the guard Calix had been playing would have been expected to show to his princess. It seemed that Calix was done with that particular pretense. Something about the thought bothered Dia but he wasn't sure what and he didn't have time to focus on it right then.

The princess's eyes narrowed slightly as they shifted from the prince to his companion.

"Who says that I haven't?"

Dia consider that for a moment, considered the princess, the queen and the webs of court intrigue that had always surrounded them both. He let out a soft breath.

"Let me guess. You keep having 'accidents' and you've guessed who's behind them, but you've never been able to prove anything?"

Emira nodded slightly, her eyes returning to him.

"What if I could help you prove it?"

At that Emira went completely still, eyes fixed on his face as though searching for the trap in his words, then, slowly, "She's after you now too, isn't she?"

Dia inclined his head. "Her current plan is to have you assassinated and make it look like I'm the one behind it, at least it was until she realized I was onto her."

Emira tilted her head to the side. "How did that happen?"

"It doesn't matter." Dia said it quickly, forcing himself not to glance at Calix. "What matters is that now she's found a way to take one of my siblings hostage without them even knowing about it and she's told me that she'll kill them if I don't kill you by noon today."

Again Emira's reaction was muted, a slight narrowing of her eyes her only response. Behind her however, Captain Omdare's hand shifted to the hilt of her blade. A moment later a flicker of movement in the corner of Dia's eye told him that Calix had mirrored the motion. Feeling the tension rise in the room Dia pressed on quickly.

"I have no intention of trying to kill you. I'm here to ask for your help. We have the same enemy. Working together I think we could set a trap that can give us the proof we need to finally be free of her. But that can't happen until my sibling is safe. If I swear to help you destroy the Qqueen, will you help me save my sibling?"

At first Emira said nothing, only looked at him, consideration in her bright green eyes. Dia met and held her gaze, willing it to show her whatever she needed to see to believe that his offer was genuine. His heart was pounding, his palms damp with sweat. If she didn't believe him… If she thought this was a trap so he could kill her and ransom Evren then…

"Which one of your siblings does she have?"

"Evren." Their name fell hoarse and cracked from Dia's lips as that simple admission brought fear for them flooding over him again. "She's holding them in the clinic apothecary."

"I see… They're an apprentice there, aren't they?"

Dia started. "You know that?"

The corners of Emira's lips curved ever so slightly. "Naturally. Technically they are my step-sibling after all."

Dia's eyes narrowed and with all the emotions swirling through him he didn't quite manage to keep the edge of accusation from his tone. "I'm surprised to hear you say that considering you never so much as speak to either of them."

If Emira was bothered by either the words or the tone nothing in her face showed it. In fact her expression actually softened slightly, a weariness creeping into her voice. "Prince, my own stepmother has been trying to destroy me since I was a child and she is far from the only one. Every person I spend time with is either a potential threat or a potential vulnerability for me."

Dia stared at her, realization beginning to dawn. "You thought they would be a weakness for you."

To his surprise the princess shook her head. "No, for you. Despite being a prince you managed to have a real family. I stole your birthright. I know that. I have no intention of giving it back, but that doesn't mean I don't owe you something for taking it. You seemed to be happy with your family. I thought the least I could do for you was to protect them by staying away."

Dia's breath caught in his throat, his eyes going wide as he took in her words, took in all they implied about their relationship, about how Emira had viewed Evren and Ruslan, had viewed him, for all these years. He had misjudged her, that was obvious. He could not blame himself for it, not when that had so clearly been her intent. He had always known that her coolness was a mask but now, for the first time, he was getting a glimpse of what lay behind it. If what he saw was true, then...

"So you'll help me?"

Emira watched him for a moment, then, slowly, she nodded.

"I'll help you."

CHAPTER 14
THE TRUTH

The cart rolled along the cobblestones, bumping slightly every time its wheels ran over a patch of uneven ground. The inside of the cart was dim thanks to the tarp thrown over it but the occasional gleam of morning sunlight still managed to make its way into the gaps between fabric and wood. Dia had hated the idea of waiting for morning, hated the idea of leaving Evren in the queen's clutches for so long, but the amount of clear space around the clinic meant that they had no choice but to approach it openly. Dia had little doubt that if he, Calix or anyone else the queen thought connected to him tried to approach either entrance Evren would die before they could get inside. Desperate as she was, the queen was also clever and that meant there was even a chance she had foreseen Dia going to Emira for help. Maybe the chance of Evren dying as soon as the princess approached the apothecary wasn't a large one, but it was still one he refused to take, and so the morning and the cart.

Dia had borrowed it and the horses to pull it from a crafter who owed him a favor for assisting them with a material supply issue a year before, and now he, Calix, and Emira crouched in its dimness. Captain Omdare sat on the box, disguised in a servant's stained tunic and worn work pants, her braid tucked under a black work cap, the brim of which shaded her face. Brown hair and suntanned skin were common features in H'arn. Between that and the disguise she was far less likely to be recognized than any of the other three. She was also the one that the guards were least likely to be watching for. Dia would have preferred to take more than one of Emira's guards with them but when he had asked her how many others she trusted, she had calmly told him "none of them." So they had agreed to keep the circle tight. Taking Evren in a public place without them even knowing might have been a masterstroke but it was also a desperation move, and it created an opening. So long as the queen didn't figure out what was about to happen, if they played things right, they could save Evren and destroy the queen all at the same time.

"Halt!" The shout came from somewhere nearby and the cart rolled to a stop. Dia tensed, itching to peer out from beneath the fabric but knowing he couldn't, not yet. Beside him he felt Calix shift into a kneeling position, ready to spring up the moment the signal came. From beyond Calix the slight creak of boards told him that Emira was also getting into position.

"What do you have here?" The voice was the same one which had told them to halt, and from the sound of multiple pairs of footsteps approaching the cart, he wasn't alone.

"Herb delivery." Captain Omdare's voice had picked up a slight accent Dia vaguely recognized but couldn't quite identify. Whatever it was, it altered the quality of her voice just enough to make it hard to recognize. "They're expecting me."

"Alright. Just step out of the cart and let us inspect it before you begin unloading."

"Inspect it?" The captain's voice rose in feigned incredulity. "Why do you need to inspect it? They've never inspected it before!"

"New safety protocol," the queen's guard, for so he must be, replied flatly.

The other guards said nothing, a fact which confirmed Dia's prediction. They must still have their ears clogged to protect them against Calix's music, while this man had been added come morning to be the ears and voice of the group. He might be susceptible to the power of Calix's pipe but the moment he started to collapse his companions would know what was happening and would no doubt signal whoever was guarding Evren. That meant they needed to handle things a different way.

There was a creaking and the thud of boots hitting cobblestone as Captain Omdare jumped down from the cart. "Safety protocol for what? This better not be an excuse to confiscate my goods without paying me!"

"I assure you, this is simply safety protocol."

"Well you would say that wouldn't you?" Even without being able to see what was happening Dia could picture the captain getting in the guards face, her eyes flashing with righteous anger.

"Ma'am, please step away from the cart."

"I will do no such thing! You, don't touch that tarp! I want to speak to one of the apothecarists!"

Dia tensed. If the ear-blocked guards were close enough to be in danger of removing the tarp then...

"Ma'am, step back or..." The guard's voice suddenly changed into a horrible gurgling noise. The signal.

Dia lunged upward, throwing off the tarp. Light flooded his eyes and he blinked rapidly, trying to get his vision to clear. It took precious seconds, but the tricksters own luck seemed to be with them because the other three guards had also paused for a moment, their eyes drawn to the sight of the small blade Captain Omdare had kept concealed in her palm, now buried in their leader's throat. The guard closest to the door recovered himself first, turning on his heel as though to race for the clinic, but by that time Calix was already moving.

The Fox threw himself over the side of the cart, the dagger flying from his hand to catch the guard in the back of the shoulder. It wasn't a mortal wound but it was enough to make the guard stumble and spin around, drawing his blade to defend himself. Calix met his blade with the short sword Dia had lent him just as another guard tried to stab the Fox from behind. Without pausing to think Dia too threw himself from the cart, tackling the guard and sending them both crashing to the ground. Pain lanced through the prince's shoulder and hip as they slammed against the cobblestones, and a grunt of pain left the guard's lips. Then he was twisting in Dia's arms, trying to rise. Dia gasped as he felt an elbow slam into his already bruised side but he clung on, digging his fingers into the back of the guard's jacket and tangling their legs as best he could. Furious, the guard shoved his elbow into Dia's side again then rolled onto his back, using his superior bulk to crush the prince beneath him. Dia hissed in pain but held on, refusing to let him up. He might not be a good enough fighter to match blades with any of these soldiers but, by the Hexium, he was going to do his part.

The guard twisted once more in Dia's grip then, suddenly, he shuddered, a hoarse gurgling noise falling from his lips, and he went limp. Beneath him, Dia panted for breath. His whole body throbbed from the struggle and he could feel a horrible warm wet something dripping onto the front of his vest and shirt.

"Prince?" The question came from just above him, the voice that of Captain Omdare.

Hastily Dia pushed the dead man off of himself and scrambled to his knees, his breath still coming quickly. His eyes flicked to the guard, catching for a moment on the crimson pooling from his throat, then hastily moving away again. His stomach twisted at the sight and the feel of the man's blood seeping through his shirt onto his skin, but he didn't have time for such weakness so he pushed it away. His eyes moved upward instead to see Captain Omdare standing above him, one bloody hand still holding her little blade, the other extended out to him. Dia took it, allowing himself to be pulled to his feet as he glanced around, taking in the carnage. The guard who had been fighting Calix was on the ground, dead, as was the fourth guard, and, standing over him with blue white light crackling over her fingertips, was Princess Emira.

Dia's eyes widened. He had known of course, everyone in the court knew. For years it had been a topic of gossip and speculation and even fear among the people of the Palace City. Lightning was a rare gift, a wild gift, hard to master and easy to misuse. Many adults who tried to tame it had ended up dead, struck down by their own gifts. Yet even knowing the danger, Queen Su Yin had left her gift to a newborn baby. 'She didn't have to,' members of the court would whisper. 'She didn't die so suddenly that she didn't have time to will it to someone else. She had cousins, friends, a sister. If she just focused on one of them when she died they could have had it instead.' Yet Queen Su Yin had not done that and her power had passed to her newborn daughter. For the first several years of Emira's life she had been fed a draft every day to keep her gift in check, but when she turned twelve she stopped taking it. That was when the murmurs had begun in earnest as those throughout the Palace City sought to avoid the Princess whenever possible, certain that it was only a matter of time before her gift got out of control and killed either her or those around her.

Yet that day had never come. How Emira had managed to control her wild gift at such a young age Dia had no idea, but somehow she had done it, keeping it locked within her so completely that no one who did not know she possessed it would ever have guessed. Now, seeing the lightning flickering across her fingertips and the dead man lying at her feet, Dia knew that her control over the wild gift was even greater than anyone had realized.

Calix bent and pulled his dagger free of his dead guard then turned to Dia.

"Are you alright?"

Dia's side throbbed where it had struck the cobblestones and he was pretty sure both it and his back would be covered in bruises come nightfall. But thanks to years of illness the prince was used to ignoring the discomfort of his body, so he just nodded.

"Are you?"

Calix sheathed his dagger.

"Fine."

Captain Omdare returned to the cart, pulling her sword from the bed and belting it back on as Princess Emira stepped around the cart to join them.

"Ready?"

Calix nodded and pulled his pipe from inside his jacket. "Let's go."

As the four of them moved to the door at the back of the clinic Dia couldn't help casting a glance back at the dead guards. They hadn't been his enemies, not really. They were merely the latest victims of the games of politics and power which were so often played within the Palace City's walls. To keep her secrets safe, the queen would not have told them more of her plans then they needed to know to do their jobs, so Dia was sure they had held no real idea what they were dying for. They had merely been ordinary people obeying their queen. Dia's eyes moved from them to the princess walking beside him, lightning still dancing at her fingertips.

"Does it bother you, killing your own men?"

Emira looked coolly back at him. "If they served the queen then they aren't *my* men."

Dia consider that for a moment, then nodded slowly. She was right of course. The men, if the queen was trusting them with this, had probably been a gift from the Warlord of the West, loyal to her and her sister, not to the Demiter line. Even so, the cold pragmatism in Emira's voice reminded him that, even if they were allies in this, that didn't make them allies in everything.

Ahead of them Calix pushed the door of the clinic open. Then Dia's unease calmed and began drifting away as the Fox put the pipe to his lips and began to play. Through the warm peaceful haze of the music Dia saw a couple of people dressed in apothecary smocks crumple to the ground, too relaxed to stay on their feet, but still awake. That was the key to this, they had to stay awake. Dia hadn't been sure if he should tell Emira about Calix's pipe or if the Fox would prefer to keep his secrets. But to the prince's surprise Calix had actually volunteered the information himself, freely explaining the power of the music and the control he had over it. Too relieved to be able to use every advantage they had to question it, Dia had incorporated the pipe into their plan, its power removing obstacles even as it created a captive audience for what was to come.

With the notes of the pipe still folding his mind in calm Dia followed Calix into the hall, finding that it was easier to move under the music's spell now when he was expecting it than it had been that first time, in the queen's garden the night before. It was still hard to think about anything besides the music but Dia did his best, eyes moving along the wooden beams of the walls and over the flickering lanterns. They had only gone a few steps when they reached a door on their right. Judging by its proximity to the back entrance it was probably a brewery or a storeroom. Still playing, Calix tilted his head at Dia in a question and the prince nodded, going to it and pushing the door open. They were greeted with the mixing scents of drying herbs and the sound of two more apothecarists slumping to the ground. Dia had been right: a storeroom. No one else was in the room, but two doors led off of it, one to the left of where they had entered and one on the opposite wall. Dia tried the one on the opposite wall first, revealing another storeroom, this one empty, then the one to the left which revealed the apothecary and beyond it the distillery.

Abstractly Dia knew that he should be starting to worry, that even if they had silenced the guards outside before they could signal any of their comrades, it was still only a matter of time before someone found the corpses lying behind the clinic and raised the alarm. Their whole plan hinged on finding Evren before anyone realized what was happening, Evren's *life* hinged on finding them before anyone realized what was happening. Every door they tried which didn't reveal his sibling should had him panicking more ... Yet it didn't. It was a strange feeling, knowing what was happening and what was at stake and yet being unable to feel the terror he ought. No matter what thoughts swirled through his mind the peace of the music still clung to him, soothing away his fears before they could properly form. He wasn't entirely sure he liked having them taken from him, yet even as that thought formed in him the distress surrounding it was soothed away as well.

There were several people in the distillery but none of them were Evren. Dia returned to the main hallway, Calix at his side and the other two just behind them, moving like dazed sleepwalkers. The next door they tried revealed a small room filled with pallets, which Dia realized must be the room where Evren and the other apprentices slept between patients during their nights on call. It was empty now that it was full morning, but there was another door on the far side of it. As Dia moved closer to it he thought he could hear the murmur of voices beyond. He gestured at Calix, who stilled for a moment then lowered his pipe. Instantly the world crashed back in, alarm and distrust, terror and anger, all striking him so fast that Dia rocked back with the force of the emotions. Judging by the widening of their eyes and the stiffening of their bodies Princess Emira and Captain Omdare were experiencing something very similar. Only Calix remained calm, his quick breaths from having played for so long seemingly his only discomfort.

"Through there?"

Dia nodded. "I think so. Since they weren't in the apothecary that probably means they're in the main ward"

"How long until the ones in the hallway come out of it?" It was the princess who asked the question.

"About half an hour. The power was directed at them, not at you."

The princess gave Calix a considering look. "You're sure they're conscious enough to remember what they see?"

Calix inclined his head. "Trust me princess, I know what I'm doing."

That earned him a particularly cold glance from Emira but then she nodded stiffly and turned back to the door. Dia approached it and took a breath. Now that the pipe's music was no longer filling him with artificial calm his mind once again buzzed with fear for Evren. What if they weren't behind this door either? What if he was wrong? Yet it only made sense that the apprentice's resting room would be just off of the main ward, so they could hear if anyone entered or called for them during the night. Taking a deep breath Dia wrapped one hand around the hilt of his belt knife and, with the other, he pulled the door open.

The ward beyond was a long room comprised of two rows of beds, each one separated from the beds surrounding it by a screen decorated with flowers and birds. Half a dozen doctors, apothecarists and apprentices moved between the beds, talking to patients or consulting with each other. The room hummed with so much activity that no one looked up when the door opened. Dia took two steps forward, eyes frantically scanning the room until he spotted a blessedly familiar head of dark wavy brown hair.

"Ev!"

Evren's head jerked up from where they were measuring some tincture into a patient's glass. They automatically tucked a strand of their wild hair back behind one ear and blinked at him in surprise.

"Dia?"

"Ev, come here, quick!"

Dia was already striding toward them, eyes scanning what he could see of the patients. Heads were turning in their direction, curious, confused, interested.

If the queen is smart about this then she'll have told her people to stand down if I get this far. But if she's really desperate enough to make a mistake then she won't want to just let Ev go. She'll want to prove to me she's serious so that when she threatens Ruslan I'll do what she wants and that means...

A flicker of movement from their left, a figure coming off their bed far too quickly for one injured or ill, a flash of silver...

"Calix!"

Instantly the melody of Calix's pipe washed over the ward, sending staff and patients alike dropping to their knees and then to the ground. Evren swayed on their feet blinking dazedly as behind them the person with the knife crumpled to the floor, the blade dropping from their relaxing grip. Dia wasn't sure if the dizziness he felt in that moment was a product of the music or purely a product of his own relief. Evren was safe. They were safe. They were going to be ok. This wasn't going to be like last time. It...

The sound of running footsteps from farther down the ward broke through Dia's thoughts and even through the calm of the music Dia felt his blood run cold, for the footsteps were not even slightly slowed by Calix's melody. He didn't need to be close enough to look to know that the woman who threw herself out from behind a screen must have something blocking up her ears. How she had managed to keep the doctors treating her from noticing something so obviously strange Dia had no idea, but it hardly mattered now. Nothing mattered except Evren wobbling toward him, slow, far too slow, his own legs, still caught in the magic of the pipe, refusing to run. The woman was gaining on Evren, the light coming through the windows flashing off of the knife in her hand...

Not again! Not again! Not again! Not Ev! Not...

"Calix STOP!"

Reality crashed back in, the dazed calm of the music shattering as the queen's guard, for so she must be, lunged for Evren. Dia threw himself forward, arms wrapping around his sibling as he tackled them. He felt a line of pain across his left shoulder as the knife meant for Evren sliced along his skin and then they were hitting the ground, Evren beneath him gasping as the impact drove all the air from their body. All of the instincts for self-defense that Dia's stepfather had trained into him were screaming at him to roll, roll away before the next strike. But with Evren confused and winded beneath him he couldn't risk it. Instead he twisted around as best he could just in time to see a flash of silver descending toward him. Still half on top of Evren Dia lunged upward, grabbing the assassin's arms, trying to hold the blade away from them.

She was stronger than he was, Dia could feel that instantly, strong with years of training, while Dia was no soldier and his body throbbed with bruises and his shoulder burned and bled. His arms shook, the knife descended, shutter to a halt, descended some more, and...

The sound of footsteps, a shadow above him, the flash of a blade. The guard let out a horrible cry and doubled over, the knife falling from her suddenly slack grip as she clutched at her stomach and the blade suddenly protruding from it. Panting, Dia looked up in time to see a heeled boot connect with the guard's gut, kicking her backward off of the blade of Dia's own short sword.

Calix.

With a shaky breath of relief Dia stared up at the Fox, at the man who had saved his life yet again.

"You're hurt." Calix extended his free hand down to Dia and the prince took it gratefully, allowing himself to be helped to his feet. He staggered slightly as he stood, pain and relief and the echo of his familiar dizziness all catching him in a single instant. Then Calix's arm was around his waist, supporting him, and for a moment Dia just let himself sag into the comfort of that touch.

"Dia?" Evren pushed themself into a sitting position, dark eyes wide with confusion. At the sight of them looking up at him, safe and whole and alive, Dia found himself pushing away from Calix so that he could drop back down to the floor and wrap his arms around his younger sibling, holding them tightly to him.

"It's alright now. Everything's going to be alright this time. I promise..."

"Dia what *is* this? What's happening?"

Dia opened his mouth, prepared to explain, to apologize, when he suddenly noticed more movement from around them, the rest of the room beginning to stir. Calix had said that those in the hall would be out of it for about half an hour. Whether it was some different intention he put into the magic here, the abruptness with which the music had been cut off, or simply some dilute effect due to the size of the room, Dia didn't know. Whatever the reason, the people in the ward around them were waking fully far sooner than he'd expected.

"Ev, how many guards are in here right now?"

Something of his sudden tension must have come through in Dia's tone because Evren didn't question him, just answered. "Five. They came in around midnight complaining of stomach pains."

Five, that meant four still alive. Straightening up on his knees Dia scanned the ward, peering between the screens as best he could, searching for threats. Far too close to them for comfort the first person who had tried to kill Evren was scrambling back to their knees, reaching for their dropped blade. One arm still wrapped around his sibling, Dia reached for his own dagger, preparing to defend them, but before he could rise the would-be killer froze, a sword coming to rest against their throat. Dia's eyes traveled up the blade to see Captain Omdare standing above them. and beside her...

"Enough!" Princess Emira's voice rang out across the ward, leaving stillness and silence in its wake. "If any here have weapons drop them *now*. If you do not you will be declared traitor and delt with accordingly." Emira prodded the dying guard lightly with her boot, cool gaze scanning the room in obvious challenge. "Do I make myself clear?"

There was silence for a heartbeat, then two, then three, and then, slowly, the sound of knives being placed upon the ground.

"Your Highness, forgive us, we were just following orders..." The person with Captain Omdare's blade pressed to their throat croaked.

"I am aware." Emira turned to stare down at the guard. "I look forward to hearing exactly what those orders were. I'm sure my father will be interested in them as well."

"Your Highnesses?" The voice came from behind them, and both Emira and Dia turned to see a man Dia recognized as one of the senior doctors walking tentatively toward them. "Forgive me for asking but ...What is happening here?"

"I would like to know that too." Evren spoke more quietly, staring up at Dia with dark worried eyes, "but before you tell me, I want to look at that cut."

As Emira moved toward the doctor, Evren gently detangled themself from Dia's embrace and shifted to examine his shoulder. Dia winced as they began pealing his vest away from the injury.

"Alright. Calix could you…" He was about to ask Calix to collect the weapons that the surrendering guards had dropped but the words died on his lips because the Fox was nowhere to be seen.

…What-

Dia blinked, realizing as he did so that he hadn't actually seen Calix since Dia moved away from him to hug Evren. When had he left? Dia hadn't noticed. He had been too distracted by everyone else in the room waking…

Distracted.

… Distraction.

Sudden unease twisted Dia's gut. Calix had said that he had some control over the effect of the music, said that he could keep people in that foggy haze for fully half an hour, yet he hadn't this time had he? No, when he played this time he'd done it in a way that let them wake almost as soon as he stopped playing.

Why?

What was Calix up to?

Why set up a distraction?

So that he could sneak away as soon as the situation began to resolve?

Why would he want to do that?

Was it because he was a spy?

Did he think Dia would turn him in as soon as Evren was safe?

Surely he must know Dia better than that?

Yes, he must know because even before they had come to their understanding Dia *still* hadn't turned him in.

So then why?

Did he need to check in or something?

No, that didn't make sense, not when he could just as easily wait a few minutes and leave openly.

Even if he was reporting everything that happened here to his handlers surely they would want to know how it ended? Surely it was better for him to witness that end than to sneak away?

No, that didn't make sense. None of this made sense. What was he missing…? What…

"Dia, what is it?" Evren was peering at him anxiously.

"Hold on." Dia pulled gently away from them and scrambled to his feet, eyes drifting aimlessly around the room, searching for some clue, some sign, and finding nothing.

"Prince?" It was Emira this time, eyes narrowing in wariness. "Is something going on?"

"It's Calix, he…" But Dia's voice trailed away, his mind and tongue catching on the name as he realized that nothing in the ward was going to give him a clue because this had nothing to do with the ward or anyone in it. This was only about Calix.

"He what?"

Dia shook his head and held up a hand in a 'wait' gesture.

This was about Calix and what did he really know about Calix? If he pushed away all of his assumptions and dealt only with the facts, what did he really know?

Calix was combat trained.

Calix had siblings but those siblings were dead.

Calix had come to the court under false pretenses.

Calix hated the Demiter line. By his own admission, he hated everyone in it except for Dia. When had that changed? When had the barbs vanished from Calix's voice to be replaced by warmth?

The day Calix had fought the assassin, the day Dia had seen his scars. ...The day Dia had shown Calix the message in blood and told him why he wanted to be king.

And suddenly it came, all the little pieces and clues falling together: The way Calix had changed after that conversation, the burn scars beneath all the other scars marking them as the oldest, the way he had fallen so easily into Dia's life, a pair of golden eyes and hair once a pale orange that must have darkened with age, the transition scars on Calix's chest, his oath to keep the king from ordering the burning of Nomenie by any means necessary, the way he had stopped playing the part of the loyal guard around Emira and why he had been so willing to tell her about his pipe as though secrecy no longer mattered...

For a moment Dia just stood there reeling as the truth crashed down over him, and then he ran.

CHAPTER 15

CALIX

The click of Calix's heels against the marble tiles of the corridor echoed in eerie counterpoint with the melody of his flute and the sound of bodies falling to the floor. Once, years ago, he had not been able to play like this without losing himself in the music too, but that had been a long time ago. Now, no matter the power of the song he played he could keep his mind clear of it. Part of him still ached to let go, to lose himself in the false peace of his own music but it was a luxury he could no longer afford to grant himself. Besides, there were things that must be done.

Before him rose the great doors of the hall of Adjra, the central throne room of the Crown. Two guards had stood before it but now they lay crumpled in sleep like all the others before them, unable to stop him.

No one could stop him now.

Not wanting to give the place the respect of taking a hand from his pipe to open the doors properly, Calix simply kicked one until it flew open, letting his song fill the hall beyond, luring its occupants into sleep.

All of its occupants save one.

King Harlin Amarth Demiter rose from his throne on the dais at the far end of the hall, stumbled a step forward, and collapsed to his knees. It was a good look for him, a look Calix thoroughly enjoyed as he slowly and deliberately crossed the space between them. Dividing his song so that all the guards and courtiers would drop into peaceful slumber while Harlin alone would remain affected but awake had taken every ounce of Calix's skill and concentration, but oh, how satisfying it was.

"Who are you?" Harlin barely managed to croak out the words, his voice a shuddering gasp.

Calix only smiled and lowered his pipe. He didn't need it anymore, not now. Now was for another weapon.

As his footsteps rang against the steps of the royal dais Calix tucked his pipe back into its pocket in his short coat and wrapped his fingers around the familiar hilt of his dagger. The dagger, the only thing he had left of the world before the blood and the burning. It had been a gift from his mothers on that final birthday, and he had loved it then for its beauty, its hilt set with precious stones. The stones were gone now, sold off long since to keep him alive. He had wrapped the hilt in leather to hide where they had been, but the dagger was still precious to him, and now, now at last he would put it to fitting use.

The sound of feet pounding on marble broke through the silence and Calix paused, glancing back over his shoulder, free hand raising in the direction of his pipe should he need it again. Then the doors of the hall crashed open once more to reveal Dia, followed closely by his sibling, the princess and the captain. Dia skidded, panting, to a stop, one hand bracing against a marble pillar as he fought for breath, and Calix allowed his eyes to linger for only a moment before he turned away again. He had thought he would have more time, but not much more. Dia was clever after all, just one of the many things Calix had always liked about him. Well, it didn't matter. Neither Dia nor any of his companions had a ranged weapon. It had still taken long enough.

"Calix! Wait!"

Calix ignored Dia's shout as he stepped toward the king.

"Dawn!"

Calix froze.

Alright, *that* he hadn't expected.

"Dawn! I know it's you! I know why you're doing this! I get it! I do! But you have to stop!"

"Why?" Calix swung around at that, his voice sharp with an anger six long, horrible years in the making. "If you know then why are you trying to stop me?"

"Because this isn't the way!" Dia pushed himself away from the pillar and took two steps toward the dais. "This will only make things worse!"

"Worse? Worse than letting him burn Nomenie to the ground?"

Dia took another step toward him, hands raised in sign of peace.

"Think about it. If he dies now the Duchy will call Emira queen, and the Warlord of the West will call Castela queen, and all of H'arn will be thrown into Civil War. There has to be another way to stop him from invading Nomenie!"

"There isn't." Calix's voice was cold. He understood Dia's desperation to find another way, of course he did. Of course he knew that Dia would never accept that this was the only answer. But it was. Oh it was.

He took a step backward and to the side until he stood beside King Harlin, gripping a handful of his hair to pull him upright and expose his throat. In his other hand Calix drew his dagger. Once, long ago he had used this very blade to spill his own blood so that he could beg Dia and H'arn to save them.

No help had come.

He knew now that it hadn't been Dia's fault, that Dia had spent his entire life trying to make amends for that one moment of helplessness, and Calix loved him for it. But that didn't change the fact that now, just as then, Dia was helpless to stop this tragedy, that now, just as then, Calix could only rely on himself.

"Calix think about it!" Dia was still talking, still trying to persuade him. "If H'arn falls to civil war think about how many people will die!"

"I know. That doesn't change what I have to do."

Calix pressed the dagger against King Harlin's throat. The man struggled weakly in his grip but the power of Calix's song still bound him more tightly than any chains. It was hopeless. The whole thing was hopeless. From beginning to end, hopeless. There would be a civil war and it would tear H'arn apart. The Crimson Age would feed again on the blood of hundreds or thousands. They would pray to their god of peace, their Star Fox, but no god would answer them, no god would save them. And it would all be his doing.

"So let the people blame me and let them die cursing my name."

The flick of a wrist, the flash of a blade, and blood splattered across the throne.

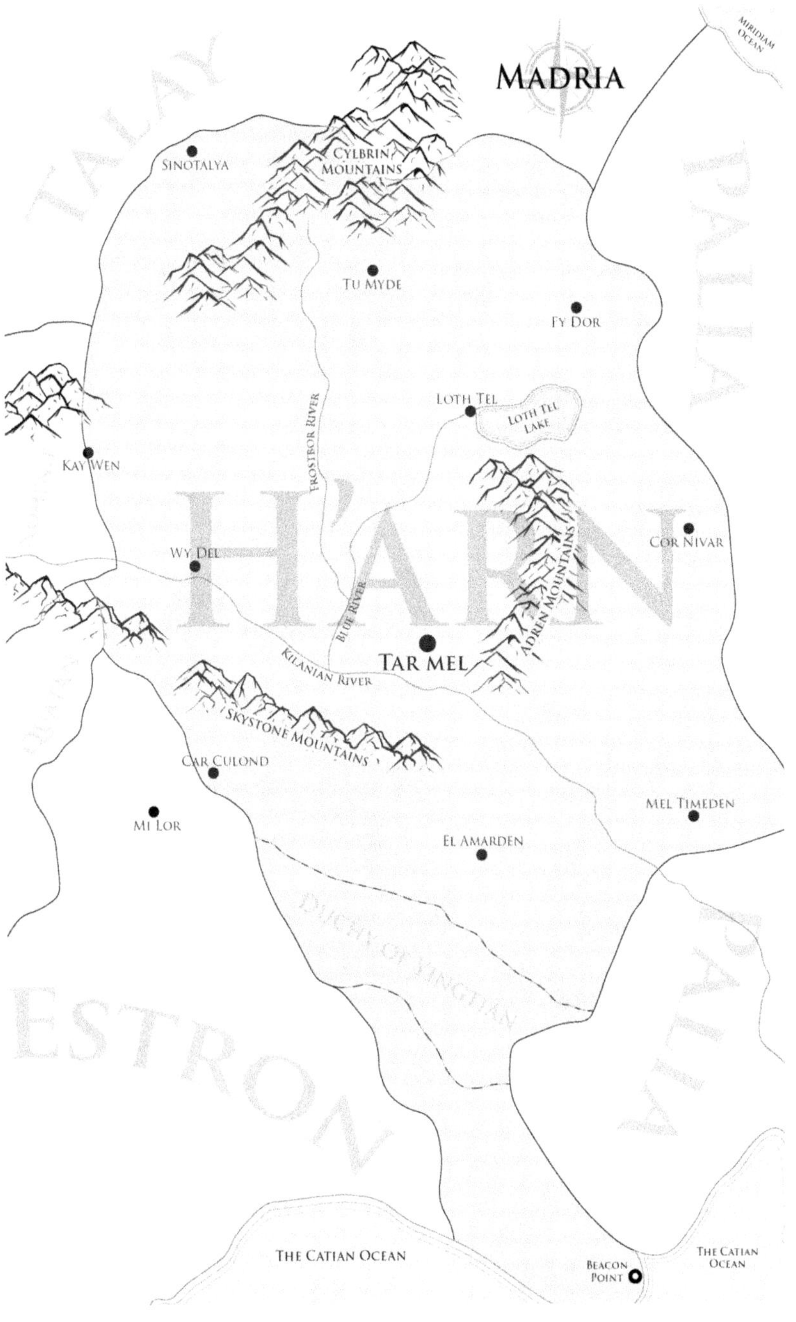

MADRIA
MIRIDIAM OCEAN
TALAY
PALIA
SINOTALYA
CYLBRIN MOUNTAINS
TU MYDE
FY DOR
FROSTBOR RIVER
LOTH TEL
LOTH TEL LAKE
KAY WEN
H'ARN
COR NIVAR
WY DEL
BLUE RIVER
ADREN MOUNTAINS
KILANIAN RIVER
TAR MEL
SKYSTONE MOUNTAINS
CAR CULOND
MEL TIMEDEN
MI LOR
EL AMARDEN
DUCHY OF YINGTIAN
ESTRON
PALIA
THE CATIAN OCEAN
BEACON POINT
THE CATIAN OCEAN

Authors Note

Yes, Calix is trans. I want to get that out of the way first. Like many trans people he didn't realize that he was not the gender he had been assigned until he hit puberty, hence the difference in how he is gendered in the prologue and Dia's childhood memories of him, versus how he is gendered throughout the book.

The world in which the book takes place is a trans-normative one. On this world, let's call it Fourth, the concept of gender is slightly different than what it is here in our reality. On Fourth there are held to be six genders, one for each combination of pronouns on a spectrum of "she" "they" and "he," each symbolized by one of the six major gods of the Hexium. This is because on Fourth the concept of gender refers to a person's pronouns without any reference to the biology they were born with. That is not to say this is a trans-perfect world. It still has the problem of gender assumptions based on appearance as a cultural norm, though not every person of any given gender conforms to the visual expectations of that gender and to misgender someone after being informed of their pronouns is viewed as among the greatest of social taboos since it dishonors the god who watches over that particular gender. This problem of gender assumptions is in the process of changing however, for, as mentioned in the book, a new trend is beginning to spread of gender correlating star sign tattoos, each star sign that of the god who watches over that gender. For anyone who is interested here is the full list.

The Trickster Cat - Chaos: They/Them

Miriam, Lady of the Storm: She/They

The Star Fox - Peace: He/They

Adjra, The Queen of Battle: She/Her

Cylbra, King of the Winds: He/Him

The Spark, The Ever-Shifting Flame: All Pronouns

As for how all of this impacts Calix's life directly: As I said before this is a trans-normative world and, as far back as records go, always has been. Because of this trans people of every variety have openly been involved in the medical sciences for as long as there have been medical sciences and many of them, throughout the centuries, have dedicated themselves to finding ways to use those sciences, as well as Fourth's unique magic, to handle problems of dysphoria. As a result the medical sciences relating to transition are some of the most advanced in the world, all of which is to say that, once he passed 16, the age of adulthood on Fourth, Calix was able to fully medically (and magically) transition which he did a couple of years before the book begins.

Now onto Dia and his illness:

The Wrong Blood Disease is what, in our world, we call Postural Orthostatic Tachycardia Syndrome or "POTS." Much like on Fourth, where it was originally incorrectly thought to be a blood disorder, our world too originally misclassified it, here as a heart disorder. In truth it is neither, but rather a disorder of the autonomic nervous system. The autonomic nervous system, a lesser-known but critical function of the human body, controls all of the nonvoluntary actions the human body performs, things like breathing, digestion, and blood circulation. POTS is a subset of the various health problems known collectively as dysautonomia or autonomic dysfunction. What is it actually like having a dysfunctional autonomic nervous system? Well, imagine letting a four-year-old run around pressing buttons in the control room of NASA and you'll get the idea.

It's common for people who have POTS to also experience other forms of dysautonomia and it's also common for POTS to vary a good deal from person to person. Some people pass out constantly, while other people spend a lot more time in the lightheaded conscious stage. Some people can continue going about their everyday lives in wheelchairs while other people need to be fully horizontal in a bed. In some people POTS is episodic and for others it isn't. As for Dia's version; that's a classic example of 'write what you know' since it's mostly drawn from the version I have.

With all that out of the way I just want to take a moment and thank all of the amazing people who have helped and supported me throughout this project, so thank you: To my friends who have been cheering me on and who have been not only supportive but also understanding of my inability to commit to being a human until after I finished this. To my beta readers whose interest, excitement, and encouragement motivated me in exactly the way I needed in order to complete this book. And especially to my mother for always supporting me, always believing in me, and for all your hard work helping me edit this. I could not have done this without you.

The Hexium Book 2: Legend of the Fox is coming summer 2025. May the Star Fox watch over you until we meet again.